FOR THE HEART OF DRAGONS

The Dragons of Eternity Series

JULIE WETZEL

To my Sister.
Although we don't always get along.
I still love you.

For the Heart of Dragons

CTP Publishing, New York

Summary: When Noah Dove, a mage with Eternity, is unable to save an ancient dragon, he is left with her dying request—save her dragon. With a bit of magic and some help from the dragon, Noah forms a Heart stone. Now the Dragon is loose… And only Kara Rose—a therapist trained to help troubled dragons—can stop it. The task will push her knowledge—and personal boundaries—to their limit and beyond.

ISBN: 978-1-63422-493-2 (paperback)
ISBN: 978-1-63422-170-2 (e-book)
Cover Design by: Marya Heidel
Typography by: Gem Promotions
Editing by: Chelsea Brimmer

Chapter 1

Glancing around the room, Noah tried to listen to the woman in front of him as she prattled on about the upcoming release from some new designer. Supposedly, the designer was making outfits dragons could shift in. It was an intriguing notion, but Noah didn't see how it could work. There was too much of a size difference between a dragon's three forms. No way could the same garment be used in all of them. He filed the information away for future investigation. It was always good to know about the new trends in the dragon world, although he—being human—would probably never wear them.

Taking a sip of the golden liquid in his champagne flute, Noah looked around at the crowd. He both loved and hated these events. A dragon gala brought out the cream of the crop in their finest, and tonight's event was no different. Every dragon who was anyone had come out to celebrate the king's birthday. Alongside the finely dressed men was an amazing array of beautiful women. There was everything from sophisticated evening gowns to barely there cocktail dresses, and Noah had a great view of them all. The drawback… He had to do it sober. It would have been so much better if the sparkling apple juice in his glass had been champagne, like the rest of the guests were drinking. But, then again, he wasn't a guest. He had a job to do.

Speaking of jobs…

Noah turned his attention inward and traced the lines of power out, feeling the protections he'd helped install. The chateau the king had chosen for the party was naturally well protected. Thick hedges of holly bordered up against the iron fences that circled the property, making it hard to get onto the grounds uninvited. But with dragons coming up missing, the king wanted no chances taken with his party guests, so six of Eternity's finest mages had gotten together and set up magical protections.

Noah had the honor of being one of those six. If honor was what you called the exhausting task. It had taken nearly twelve hours to set the magical circle that could be raised in an instant to keep out an attacking force. The circle also monitored anything of power that crossed it. The mages had spent the first part of the party watching the only gate into the grounds, vetting each source of magic that crossed the line, and there had been quite a few. Each dragon that entered raised a warning flag. That had been expected. What had not been expected was the number of magical items the guests had brought. Glamour spells had been everywhere. It seemed every young lady had some small trinket to enhance her beauty in some way or another. But even the slightest traces of magic had to be checked.

Just a few weeks ago, Daniel—the head of Eternity—had brought in a small medallion to be studied. Only a few of the top mages had even seen the item. Noah had been one of the few who had been able to touch and study it. The magic on the item was weak, but it did strange things. The few dragons who had touched the amulet complained that there was a distance between their human and dragon selves. Sometimes, the space would fade quickly. Other times, it would linger long enough to keep the dragon in question from shifting between forms for a while. Unfortunately, the spell faded away before they could determine exactly what it did.

As the only human mage in that select group, Noah had spent most of his time handling the necklace so the others could study it without being affected by its power. That led to some long hours in the lab. Thankfully, the medallion's power only burned through some of the dye he had used to color his hair. His Irish red hair was kissed with the silver that marked him as a human who used heavy magic—a stigma he tried very hard to hide. Thankfully, he had found a place that accepted him and his talents.

"Are you listening to me?"

The voice of the young lady in front of him broke into Noah's thoughts. For a moment, he had forgotten she was there.

"Yes." He smiled at her warmly, trying to recall what she'd been rambling on about. "I can't see how that's going to change fashion trends," he said, hoping she was still on the topic of the new garments and hadn't moved on to something else while he'd been distracted.

"Oh, but it will!" She went on about some new type of material that was going to be used in next year's line of gowns.

Noah let out a sigh of relief as he nodded at her encouragingly. The one-track mind of this debutante had saved him from a very awkward explanation. He was supposed to be blending in with the crowd, watching for hazards that may have slipped past the guards at the gate, not exposing the fact that he was security. He was also supposed to be circulating through the guests, but this young lady had latched on to him harder than most. Apparently, the silver in his hair had convinced her he was an older, distinguished gentleman. Well, that and the finely tailored tuxedo he was sporting. In truth, the lady was probably double his age. She was, after all, a dragon. They aged much slower than humans did. It was one of the few things Noah envied about dragons. That, and the whole fire-breathing, flying thing. There were very few people out there who didn't envy the ability to shift into another form. But that was a thought for another time.

Looking up, Noah caught the eye of another of Eternity's security guards circling the floor. *Demarco*. Noah nodded his head slowly at the lady in front of him, and Demarco nodded back. There was an understanding between the men that if any of them should get caught in an unwanted position, another would come and help get them out. Noah was glad when the chocolate-skinned dragon stepped up beside the young woman.

"Pardon me, my lady." Demarco flashed a wide smile when she turned to look at him. "I couldn't help but notice your gown. Is that a Josephine Del Piña?"

"Why yes, it is!" The young girl beamed at him.

Noah covered his smile with the rim of his glass as he took a sip. It was just like Demarco to be up on the latest designers on the market. After all, the man had probably spent hours with the rest of the security detail studying how one could hide weapons in designer gowns.

As Demarco drew the woman into a conversation on the pros and cons of metal-boned corsets, Noah slipped away unnoticed. He let out a sigh of relief and disappeared into the crowd. Most of the time, he could get his job done while using one of the young ladies in the group as cover. The goal was to find one that was slightly self-centered or flighty. Once he got her going, he would nod mindlessly at her words while searching the crowd for danger. Then, once he was done, he would excuse himself and move on to another area. But every now and then, he would get one that noticed when he zoned out to do his job. Like the woman he'd just escaped.

Looking around, Noah found a passing waiter and set his unfinished glass of juice on the waiter's tray. The sparkling liquid wasn't sitting well in his stomach. Besides, there were more important things to do than pretend to be a guest. Finding an empty space near one of the stone columns, Noah leaned against the marble support and closed his eyes. He relaxed his mind and whispered the spell he needed to search the room.

Colors burst inside his head as he reached out into the astral plain. Auras of the people surrounding him washed over him for a second before he came to grips with the change in his perspective. Even though it took him a moment to get used to this view, he loved it. The colors of people's auras were just as amazing as the fancy gowns the ladies wore. But they told a lot more about the intent of the wearer than their finery. Reds and golds of happy people swirled around him as he relaxed against the pole. A hint of blues and greens from the bored guests speckled the group. Two pools of intense purple shone brightly.

Noah cracked open his eyes and searched for the owners of the auras. Intense colors usually showed someone with a purpose. The first belonged to a young woman. Her eyes were locked on a young man. It was clear she was trying to work up the courage to talk to him. That, he could ignore. The second was from a pair of men deep in what seemed like a passionate conversation. It was probably some business deal going down, but there was no harm in checking.

Glancing around, he found what he was looking for—an Eternity agent watching him. This was a very common thing at these parties. It was, after all, his job to search for threats. He almost never intervened in them, however. Nodding to the security guard, he glanced at the men in question. It wasn't hard to point out the pair. The men's passionate conversation was growing rather heated. The agent nodded and went off to defuse the situation before it exploded.

Drawing in a soothing breath, Noah closed his eyes and searched the room again. He couldn't afford to miss anything important. A soft aura of green washed up along his side, drawing his attention. Opening his eyes, Noah looked at the man who had settled against the column next to him. A smile curled the corner of Noah's mouth as he recognized the man. "Hello, Laurence."

"Finding anything interesting?" Laurence asked as he looked down into his glass of sparkling apple juice.

Noah straightened up as a full smile graced his lips. Laurence was Noah's partner in crime. Daniel usually always paired them together when they were sent out on missions. Laurence was taller than Noah by nearly a full head, and that was saying something since Noah was every bit of six feet tall. Laurence was also built like a tree—stout and round, but without an ounce of fat on him. Noah, on the other hand, was long and lean with broad shoulders. During their very first mission together, they had come to an agreement. Noah would stay out of the actual action and chuck spells from the sidelines while Laurence pummeled the crap out of whatever Noah took down. It was an arrangement that had worked well for both of them over the years.

"Nothing too interesting."

Laurence made a disappointed noise in his throat. "Well, you had better not stand here for too much longer. You looked like you were ready to fall asleep." There was a touch of humor in the warning. "You don't want that getting back to the boss."

Noah chuckled and stood up fully. "You're right." He released the spell and blinked the last traces of it away. "Heaven forbid Daniel think I was napping on the job." Amusement colored his words.

One unlucky soul had been caught falling asleep at an event like this before, and the poor man was still out guarding an empty flagpole. And would be for the foreseeable future.

"Would you like to walk?"

Laurence laughed and stood up. "Gladly." The pair turned and made their way through the guests. "It looks like it's going to be a nice, quiet party." He sighed in disappointment.

"Looks like it," Noah said with a chuckle. Laurence was a good man, but he liked action. His dragon was huge and liked to be right in the middle of any fight he could find. That trait carried over into his human form.

"Oh well." Laurence let out a snicker. "At least the king will have a nice, quiet birthday. Unlike the last event."

A grimace stole across Noah's face. That had been a total fiasco. Somehow, someone had gotten in to Baron Estivis's ball and kidnapped the king's sister right under all of their noses. Thankfully, Noah had been off that day. Those poor men had been sent back to basic training. And the instructors were not being easy on them.

Magic tingled up Noah's spine, and he stopped in his

tracks. Something powerful had just crossed the barrier spell.

Noticing Noah's sudden attention shift, Laurence stopped and looked around. "Something's up?"

"Maybe." Noah turned and made his way across the room to the doorway. He wasn't sure where the other mages were, but something powerful was coming.

"Finally." Laurence grinned as he set his drink down on one of the waiters' trays as they passed. "So what is it?" The man cracked his knuckles.

"Not sure," Noah said as he pushed his awareness out, feeling for the power. There was a low hum of energy around him, but there was definitely something outside.

He and Laurence had just made it to the foyer when the double doors opened and a woman stepped in. She was the most gorgeous creature Noah had ever seen. Long locks of raven-black hair spilled over her shoulders and fluttered down over her ample chest. Though there was plenty of material in the black satin dress she wore, it was cut so it left nothing to the imagination, hugging her body in a way that made Noah's fingers twitch to touch it. The long skirt of the dress pooled on the floor around her, but there was a split in it that went clear to her hip. Her dark eyes landed on the pair of men and stuck there. The sway in her walk sent unexpected shivers of desire through Noah. He shook his head, trying to clear the sudden array of X-rated images that swarmed his brain.

A hand came down on Noah's shoulder, stopping him in his tracks.

"Get her out of here," Laurence hissed.

Noah looked up at his companion. "Why?" he asked, unsure what to do. He had never known Laurence to balk at any task, but here he was, scared by a woman. And the look in his wide eyes was definitely fright.

"That's Raven Nightingale," Laurence whispered. His eyes were trained on the approaching woman.

Noah nodded and looked back at Raven. The name was familiar to him. She was a powerful dragon mage. She was also one of the oldest dragons known to exist. But that was no reason to fear her. Noah had always heard she was a very pleasant person. The hand on his shoulder tightened to a painful degree.

"She's fertile."

Panic rose in Noah. Any female dragon in their fertile period could cause problems. An old dragon was even worse. When they hit their fertile period, they could drive an entire room full of male dragons into a brooding. And here they were—an old, fertile female dragon in a room full of males. No wonder Laurence was freaking out.

"Yes," Noah said and stepped out from under the hand on his shoulder. He needed to stop her before she got into that room, and Laurence was not going to be of any help.

"At *any* cost!" Laurence hissed.

Noah didn't see his friend turn and race off, but there was no doubt that the man was on his way to find Daniel. Drawing himself to his full height, Noah pulled on a friendly smile and walked up to meet Raven. He could feel her eyes burning into him as he approached. "Good evening, my lady," he said as he barred her path into the gala.

She stopped in front of him. Her eyes traced his frame. "Are you Eternity?" She cocked her head, considering him.

"Yes." There was no reason for him to hide his identity from her.

Raven drew in a long breath, smelling the air. "Are you human?"

"Yes."

There was a long pause as she considered him. "Are

you… single?"

Thrown by the question, Noah stared at her for a second before his brain kicked into gear. "Yes?" he said, confused. *Why does she want to know if I'm single?*

She paused for a moment longer before making some decision. "You'll do." Reaching out, she grabbed Noah by the belt at the front of his pants and started pulling him towards the door.

"My lady!" he squeaked, shocked by her actions. He planted his feet, stopping her.

Turning around, Raven looked at him. "Or would you rather I make my choice from the men in the other room?"

"No!" The word echoed through the foyer, carried by several voices.

Noah glanced back at the men blocking the way into the larger room. They were all agents of Eternity. They were all dragons. And they all looked terrified at the prospect of letting this woman into the building. Surprised by their actions, Noah turned back to Raven. Indecision ate at him.

"Don't you find me attractive?" she asked as she closed the distance between them. The hand holding his belt dropped lower and rubbed against the bulge that had grown in his pants.

Shocked, Noah grabbed her hands and pulled them away. How could she be fondling him in public like that? Better yet, how come he was already hard? Sure, he liked women, but it usually took more than a skimpy dress to turn him on like that.

"Just go," Josh called from the line of men behind him. "We'll take care of things here."

"Yes, come," Raven purred as she rubbed her chest into Noah's body. "They have this."

Desire washed over Noah as he wrapped his arms

around the wanton woman.

She rumbled a contented note and slipped her wrists from his fingers. "And I'll see that you're *well* taken care of." Her hands slipped under his arms and up his back. "Just let me worry about everything for a while."

Torn between duty and desire, Noah shivered as need wracked his frame. He had never had a woman affect him as much as Raven did. The irresistible urges from his body and the insistent encouragement from his coworkers made up his mind, and he nodded his agreement.

The purr rumbling from Raven dropped in tone, vibrating deeper into his body. "Good." She leaned up and bit him on the neck. Not hard enough to break skin, but still hard enough to leave a mark. It drove a shudder through him as his knees nearly gave way. "You are mine."

Noah breathed hard as he leaned against Raven. A little voice in the back of his head yelled that he was making a huge mistake, but it was erased by the feel of her in his arms. Any protests he could have made didn't matter anymore. He belonged to her now. He would do what she asked. No matter what.

"Come," she purred as she pulled out of his arms.

A whimper slipped out of Noah at the loss of her touch.

She took his hand and led him out the front door.

Giving in to the need riding him, he tugged her to his side and wrapped his arm around her waist as they went down the short steps.

She moaned in response and leaned into him. Taking his free hand, she draped it across her chest so he held her as they walked.

Whatever warning voice that had been going off in his head died a silent death as she pressed his palm into her breast. Desire burned through what little restraint he had left, and his feet stalled on the path to the gate. Turning Raven in his arms, he crushed her against him as his lips descended to catch hers. The fact that he stood in front of the king's birthday party with half of his coworkers watching made no difference to him. The only thing that mattered was the woman in his arms and the fact that there was too much clothing between them. His fingers found the top of her bodice, and he ripped it down, exposing her to the night air.

She threw her head back and laughed in delight.

Noah growled at the loss of her mouth and attacked the side of her neck with a line of kisses and bites. He bent her backwards as he worked his way down to the sensitive skin he'd exposed.

"Raven!"

The sound of Daniel's voice cut through some of the lust riding his brain, making Noah pull back from the creamy skin he'd been worshiping. He turned just in time to see his boss storm down the few steps from the door to the ground.

"How dare you come here at such a time and steal one of my men!"

"Hello, Daniel," Raven purred as she leaned in against Noah. "I don't know what you mean." She wrapped her arms around him, holding him to her. "He came willingly."

Noah felt Daniel's eyes run over him. He wanted to stand up, away from the woman rubbing against him, but he couldn't draw the willpower to break their connection. He opened his mouth to explain the situation, but nothing came out.

"Shhh," Raven soothed him before turning her attention back to Daniel. "You're upsetting him."

"Release him!" Daniel growled.

Release him? Those words echoed around in Noah's head, breaking into the fog that had collected there. Some sense came back to him. *What the hell is going on?* He glanced down at the woman in his arms. He vaguely remembered her mouth on his neck, but that had been inside. How had they gotten outside?

"Shhh." Raven reached up and ran her hand along his cheek, tilting his head down so he would look into her dark eyes. "You're mine."

The fog filtered back into Noah's brain, smothering his thoughts. His arms wrapped tighter around Raven, pulling her into him again.

Daniel growled at her but stopped several feet away. "Release him," he demanded.

This time, Noah just stared at him blankly. *Why is Daniel making such a fuss?*

Raven twisted in his grip so she was facing Daniel. "Would you rather I go back in and take my pick of the male dragons inside?"

Noah moaned a protest. He did not like that idea at all.

"You would never get past me and my men," Daniel challenged her.

Raven laughed. "Very well, you can have your man back, but I *will* find me a man tonight. Even if I have to hit every club downtown. And you had better be sure I'll take my sweet time about choosing."

Daniel snarled. "So you're threatening me?"

"Not a threat," Raven said cheerfully, "a promise."

"Damn it, Raven," Daniel cursed at her, "Noah's a good man. I can't stand to lose him."

Raven scoffed at him. "That was an accident." Her voice held a hint of shame in it. "Anyway, I'm too old to deal with the whims of a mate. That's why I chose a human this time. I just need him for a little while. I will see he is returned to you no worse for wear and properly rewarded."

Daniel bristled at the woman's words. "I am not running a *brothel* for you to pick and choose from as you please!"

Noah felt the woman in his arms tense as she worked herself up for a fight. His mind was still hazy with lust, but their argument had cleared it somewhat. If Daniel pushed her, she would make good on her threat. If Raven went clubbing as she was, she would drive all the male dragons in the clubs into a brooding. There would be chaos in the streets for days. He could stop that by simply going with her and being her plaything for the next few days. Either choice would mean a few days of chaos for him, but only one would save Daniel and Eternity a bunch of headache.

"I'll go." The words were out of his mouth before the pair of dragons could throw down.

Daniel stopped and stared at him. "You know what this means?"

Noah nodded his head. He didn't know exactly what he was getting himself into, but it had to be better than running riot control on brooding dragons. "I'll deal with it."

Daniel stared at them for a long minute. Noah could see the indecision in his eyes. He was weighing the same choices that Noah had.

"*Fine!*" He snapped the word so hard that his teeth clicked together. "But I want him to check in every day at noon. To me. *Directly!*" He pinned Raven with angry eyes. "And if he doesn't make that call, I will *personally* show up at your door with a SWAT team and remove him. Forcefully, if I have to. Do I make myself clear?"

Raven rolled her eyes. "Such dramatics," she grumbled.

"*Am I clear?*"

"Yes," Raven answered in an exasperated voice.

"Then take him and get the hell out of here!" Daniel snapped again.

Shaking her hair back from her face, Raven stepped out of Noah's arms. She turned around to face him and shifted forms. Black scraps of satin fluttered to the ground from her ruined dress.

Noah looked up at the massive, black dragon in awe. Her scales glittered as the light from the chateau reflected off her hide. She bent at the knee and lowered her head so Noah could climb on to her back. A hand landed on Noah's shoulder, pulling his attention back to Daniel.

"I *will* come if I don't hear from you by noon," he warned. "I just pray that it's not too late."

Noah swallowed hard as fear raced through him. He'd never seen Daniel so worried about sending one of his men on a mission before. *Are fertile females that scary?* He paused for a moment, reconsidering his decision.

Raven turned her head to look at him out of one glistening eye. She gurgled at him.

Confirming his choice, Noah stepped away from his boss and climbed onto the back of the dragon. He had flown with dragons many times, but they usually carried him in their claws. This was the first time he had ridden on the back of one. Supposedly, it was a great honor to be allowed on a dragon's back. What did that say about the woman taking him or the choice he had made? He wasn't sure, but the moment she spread her wings and kicked into the air, he wished that she had clutched him in her claws. He held on to her neck for dear life as she beat the air into submission. It was the most harrowing experience he had ever had. *If this is just the start of the week, what is the rest of it going to be like?*

Chapter 2

The soft rustle of material pulled Noah from the depths of his dream. His mind worked on the noise while his body clung to sleep. The material moved again, but this time, the edge of the bed he was on dipped down under someone's weight.

"Wake up, lover," Raven's soft voice called to him. Her hand pushed into his hair before stroking down his cheek to his exposed shoulder.

He moaned and shifted under her soft caress. Opening his eyes, he found his beautiful, dark-eyed captor staring at him.

"Good morning," she said before leaning over and claiming his lips for a soft kiss.

Reaching up, he wrapped his arms around her and pulled her more deeply into the embrace. For the last three days, from the time he woke until he passed out from sheer exhaustion, he had worshipped at this goddess's body. His only waking rest had been the few minutes around noon when he was allowed to call and reassure Daniel that he was still alive. Even mealtimes had been laced with lust and desire.

Pulling from his kiss, Raven nipped at his lip before putting some space between their bodies. "Enough of this for now, my lover," she said, reaching down and fondling his morning arousal. "I hate to leave you wanting, but I have other pressing matters this day." Letting out a forlorn sigh, she squeezed him firmly before releasing him and sitting up. "We will get back to this later."

Noah chuckled as he sat up. "As you like."

An angry growl echoed from her chest as she reached over and shoved him back down. Her long, flowing dress pulled painfully tight over his waist as she straddled him, pinning him to the mattress. Grabbing his wrists, she stretched his hands up above his head and crushed his mouth with hers. After a moment, she relented and pulled back but held him pinned to the bed.

"What I would like is to take you to the skies and teach you things that would blow your mind." Her dark eyes shifted back and forth between his. "If only you were dragon." She let out a heavy breath and climbed off him. "But Daniel would have my hide if he lost another man to my guiles."

Standing up, she turned towards the door leading out of her bedchambers. "I've left clothing in the bathroom. Wash and dress. My guests will be here shortly." She paused in the door and looked back at him. "But have no doubt, lover. As soon as they are gone, you are mine once more." With that, she slipped from the room, closing the door behind her.

Dropping his head back to the bed, Noah lay where Raven had left him for several long moments, processing what had just happened. Her words played in his head. This whole thing was supposed to be about satisfying her needs during her fertile period. Nothing more. She had made it very clear that sex was all she wanted from him—even to the point that she refused to call him by his name. But, here she was, wishing he were dragon so she could take him for aerial sex. That statement confused the hell out of him.

Having worked with a bunch of macho guys, the topic of sex and kinks often came up, usually while they were waiting for something to happen or to take the edge off a serious situation. On one occasion, the dragons had gotten into a heated conversation about intercourse in dragon form. There had been lots of opinions, but they all agreed on one thing. You only took to the skies with someone you trusted completely. The few who had tried it admitted it was a thrill like nothing else, but it was insane to do. Losing one's self in passion as you plummeted at thirty-two feet per second was sure to get your blood pumping, but doing it with someone that didn't personally care about your safety was insane. More than one dragon had met a very messy end that way. Most refused to even attempt the feat with anyone less than a bonded mate. It made Noah think two things—either Raven was an insane thrill seeker, or her feelings for him ran much deeper than he cared to think about.

Shaking his thoughts away, Noah pulled himself from the bed and went to wash. Now he knew why Daniel had been concerned with letting him go with Raven. The intensity of their time together was enough to entice anyone away from their normal life. A brooding dragon wouldn't stand a chance. He wasn't a dragon, but if she started showing him even the slightest bit of emotional attachment, he would be lost to her charms as well. At least he wasn't being driven insane by instincts that he couldn't control. Well, not *completely* insane.

NOAH STOOD at the sink and stared at the outfit Raven had left for him. The pants, if you could call them that, were two pieces of dark material sewn together at the crotch. The top of the garment was hemmed with two drawstrings that would wrap around the waist to hold it in place. It would allow him to be decent in front of guests, but a simple tug on either of the ties would have him exposed in a heartbeat. That he could handle. It was what else she had left for him that gave him a moment of pause. *Cuffs*.

Four heavy leather cuffs sat on the counter, waiting for his wrists and ankles. Picking up one of the cuffs, Noah considered it. The stiff leather was textured with hand-stamped dragon scales and waxed to a high shine. Two small silver buckles held the cuff in place, while a single D-ring would allow it to be secured to something else. He inspected the straps and found there was no wear on the leather at all. Brand new.

A smile turned the corner of Noah's mouth as he slipped the first band in place. It was cut to his size, but he buckled it as loose as he could so he could slip free if he wanted to. Raven would probably fix it later, but there was no harm in trying. Lashing the rest of the cuffs into place, he picked up the pants to complete the ensemble. A loud clunk echoed through the bathroom. Looking down, Noah found something he hadn't seen. *A collar*. It was made of the same black leather as the cuffs, but it was different. There was no heavy ring attached to it. Picking it up, Noah looked at the design tooled into its surface—a dragon with its wings spread. His heart jumped as he studied the piece.

Setting the collar on the counter, Noah put the pants on as he thought. There was only one hole in the leather, and there was no wear around the mark at all. Plus, it looked to be perfectly sized for him. Could Raven have had this made just for him? And if so, what was she saying with the gift? This wasn't a collar used to control like often used in bondage. This was something used to claim. Lifting the collar, he ran his finger over the dragon as he left the bathroom. His heart pulsed as he considered his options.

The placement of the collar gave the item's meaning more weight. Had Raven put it on top of the pile—the obvious place to put such a thing—he would have assumed it was just part of the ensemble and put it on without thinking about it. But she had placed it on the bottom, where he would find it *after* he had already gotten dressed. That action spoke volumes to the significance of the collar. It meant he had a choice if he wanted to wear it or not. Or, he could just be reading too much into a simple act. Taking a deep breath, he slipped the collar around his neck and buckled it in place.

Magic tingled over his skin, answering his question. *There is significance to the collar.* Reaching up, he pulled the collar off. The tingle stopped as the leather slipped from his skin. Looking down at the piece, he probed the leather softly to see what magic she had wrought. *A binding spell.* Noah swallowed hard as he stared at the collar. He had seen spells like this used to join a human and dragon without the need to share a scale. There was an elegance to the work that awed him. It was so simple that a child could break it, yet strong enough to allow them to share their essence. *Interesting.* Then there was the way she had left it for him.

The fact that she had practically kidnapped him when they first met colored everything they did together. She had both physically and mentally coerced him into going with her. By leaving him wanting and sending him to shower, she had given him time for whatever chemicals that may have been in his system to dissipate. His head was clear of any effect she had on him physically. By leaving the collar among his things, she'd taken away any mental pressure he may have perceived in anything she may have said while giving it. There hadn't been words of love between them, but the act of leaving the collar spoke of her position on the subject. He knew exactly what she was doing.

If he left the collar, she would say nothing of the gift and they would go their separate ways once their time together was up. Accepting the gift would show he was willing to accept her. But there was another side to the coin. The fact that the spell was fragile showed this wasn't a choice he would have to live with forever. Refusing her was permanent. Accepting her gave him options—a chance to discuss what the future could hold.

A smile slipped across Noah's face as he wrapped the leather back around his neck and secured it into place. In his short time with her, he had learned a lot about Raven. Not only was she creative and caring, she was highly intelligent. He would be a fool to pass up the opportunity to really get to know her. She had opened that door with the collar, and he was going to take it.

Pulling himself to his full height, he considered his reflection in the full-length mirror in the corner. The black of the outfit made his toned chest look paler than usual. Frowning, he ran his fingers through his auburn and silver hair. If he were going to stay with Raven, he probably should risk the freckles and see if he could get a little more color into his skin. A quick shake of his head drove those thoughts out of Noah's head. Raven didn't care that he was pale. She had already accepted him as he was, so there was no reason to worry about that part of his appearance. Now, he just had to go and play whatever part she wanted him to for the company she had mentioned. They could talk about the collar and its meaning later.

Stepping out of the bedroom, Noah felt the tingle of magic ghost across his skin. "Raven?" he called as he headed down the hall. Something wasn't sitting right in the pit of his stomach. The magic was vaguely familiar, but he couldn't place it. Following the pull of it, Noah made his way through the winding halls of Raven's home to a downstairs sitting room. "Raven?" He pushed the door open to find her resting in one of the armchairs, staring off into space. "*Raven?*" he called as he rushed to her, concerned. She didn't move as he reached out and touched her face.

A hard object slammed into his shoulder, knocking him off balance. He cursed to himself as he twisted to face his attacker. Surprise flashed through Noah. He knew his attacker! *What is he doing here with that blackjack?* Before Noah could voice his thoughts, the end of the metal rod came down and dropped him into unconsciousness.

SWIRLS OF COLOR shimmered behind Noah's eyes as the pain in his head echoed out his heartbeat. *What the hell happened?* Shifting his head, he opened his mouth and breathed through the pain, praying the contents of his stomach would stay down. He pushed down the nausea and focused on things outside the ball of agony that made up his head and shoulders.

He was alive. That much he was sure of, but the fact that he couldn't move much worried him. He shifted around and found that he was bound by the cuffs he had donned earlier. Pulling against them, he was pleased to see that one side was still loose. Relaxing, he cracked his eyes. Light stabbed into his head, and he squinted to block some of it out. The rich tones of a highly polished, wooden floor filled his field of vision. He blinked several times until things came into focus properly.

Turning his head just slightly gave him a view of the rest of the room. A table sat in the middle of what could have been a dining room, but the chairs were nowhere to be seen. Instead, three people stood around the table in long black robes. They swayed to the rhythm of some archaic chant that Noah couldn't make out. The pulse of building magic filled the room and swelled as their voices grew in strength. The heaviness of the power added to the swirling in Noah's stomach, and it was all he could do not to throw up. Whatever spell the mages were using stemmed from a branch of magic that Noah seldom touched. Blood magic.

Careful not to draw attention to himself, Noah slipped his hand free of the leather cuff. Thankfully, the mages were deep in their spell and didn't notice as their prisoner bent his legs up and worked the buckles on his ankles free. Relaxing back into position, Noah slowly shifted so he could see what the men were doing. They were focused on something spread out on the table. Fear shot through Noah's heart as he recognized the hem of the gown hanging over the edge of the table. *Raven.*

The mages' chanting had reached a fervent pitch, and the power hummed along Noah's spine. Whatever spell they were working was coming to a head, and he had but moments to do something before they completed their task. And blood magic was never used for anything good.

Focusing on the two men closest to him, Noah drew in some of the loose energy floating around the room. He shivered as the dark taint in the magic hit him. The spell being performed was strangely familiar, but Noah couldn't place it. Pushing that from his mind, he wrapped the gathered magic to his needs and launched himself at the men. Grabbing them by the shoulders, he yanked them away from the table and let loose a bolt of electricity. The well-practiced spell slipped from him with ease and dropped the men with barely a crackle of sound.

The silver flash of a knife in motion caught Noah's eye, and his heart dropped as he watched the third mage plunge the sharp point deep into Raven's chest. Shock and overwhelming rage slammed into him, and he dropped the two men from his hands. An unholy sound ripped its way out of his chest as he launched himself over the table at the last man.

Surprised by the sudden attack, the mage ripped the dagger from Raven's chest and stumbled backwards as Noah flew towards the man's throat. He raised the knife to defend himself, but Noah ignored it. The tip of the blade caught Noah in the chest just over his heart, but the man was obviously not used to hand-to-hand combat. The blood-soaked dagger slipped from the man's hand as Noah crashed into him, and the pair went down to the floor.

There was a sickening crunch of ribs breaking as Noah landed on the man's chest. His hands were already around the mage's throat, crushing the life from him. Unable to control the rage sweeping through him, Noah slammed the injured man's head into the ground twice, crushing part of his skull.

Noah sat on the dead man for a moment, panting as fury burned within him. The sudden desire to mutilate the man's body pounded at him. Ripping the dagger from his chest, he slammed it into the mage, pinning his body to the floor, but pushed the urge to do more damage away. There was something more important that needed his attention at the moment. Turning, he looked up to Raven laid out on the table. She looked as if she were asleep, but the blood flowing from the wound in her chest ruined the image.

Fear raced through him, and he scrambled up from the floor to her side. Pressing his hand over the cut, he tried to staunch the heavy flow of blood. His gut clenched as he felt the cut under his hand. The wound was deep and fell directly over her heart.

"Raven," he called softly as he touched her cheek with his free hand. He had to wake her up. "Raven!" he said again as he patted her cheek. Pain squeezed at his heart as dread filled him. "*Raven!*" he cried loudly, desperate to get her to wake. He gave her a soft shake, hoping the movement would register in her mind.

She moaned softly and shifted her head.

A tiny spark of hope glimmered in the despair that was setting in. "Come on, lover," he coaxed, trying to get her to wake.

A groan of pain came out as she moved.

"Be still, lover," Noah soothed as he pressed on the wound. He whispered the one healing spell he knew. It slowed the bleeding, but it wasn't nearly strong enough to repair the damage.

Raven let out a pained laugh as she reached up and covered his hand. "Nothing you can do can fix this, lover."

"I can try, damn it!" Noah concentrated on the wound and willed it to heal. He was a powerful mage who could pick apart trap spells and hurl fire bolts all day long, but healing was not his forte. Knitting together flesh was one thing, but this wound went clear to her heart. The fact that she wasn't dead already spoke volumes of her strength of will.

"Noah."

The use of his name drew his attention from his work, and he looked up into her dark eyes. In the entire time he had been there, it was the first time his name had graced her lips.

She smiled at him. "Thank you."

"*No!*" Noah turned his attention back to the wound and pressed on it harder, determined to save her. There was no way he was going to let her die on him. He could feel the spell that bound them together. It was still strong. If she were truly dying, that bond would be weakening. She gasped in pain as he worked, but he could feel her life slipping away under his fingers.

Reaching up, she touched his cheek, turning his face to look at her. The distant look in her eyes drove shards of ice deep into Noah's heart. "I love you," she whispered as she stroked his skin. "Save the dragon." Drawing in one final breath, she shuddered as the life drained from her.

Noah caught her hand before it could slip away from his skin. Tears poured down his face as he clutched her hand in his. "*No!*" he screeched. Grabbing her limp body, he dragged it off the table and folded her into his lap on the floor. Her life was gone, but he could still feel power in her body. He held her to him, chanting every spell he could think of. Nothing helped.

Slowly, his rage subsided into despair. She was gone. Soul-deep pain like he had never known ripped through him. Throwing his head back, he screamed out his loss. True, he had only known her a few days, but those days had been intense. Tears slipped down his face as he held her, thinking of what could have been. He had accepted her bonding, but he never got to experience what it meant. His fingers rose to the buckle at the back of his neck. Without her, there was no reason for him to keep the spelled collar on.

"No!"

A voice rang through Noah, making him gasp. He

clutched at his head as the world waved in and out of focus.

"Save me!"

Noah swallowed hard as he sat up and looked around for the source of the call.

"Save me!" it cried again.

Noah clutched his ringing head. "Where are you?" he called out.

"I am here. Save me." The call came again, but this time it was a desperate whisper that continued to repeat in his head.

Something powerful needed his help. Closing his eyes, Noah pushed his emotions away and listened with his heart. In his calmer state, he found the trickle of power whispering to him and followed it to the woman in his arms. Opening his eyes, he looked down at her lifeless body. *How can she be calling out? She's dead.*

"She is. I am not," the voice answered him.

Noah studied her for a moment. There was definitely no life in her, but there was still power. "Who are you?"

"I was hers. We are bound. You are mine. Save me!"

Working this over in his mind, Noah thought about it. The only binding he could remember was the collar that bound him to Raven and her dragon. The epiphany rang through Noah's soul. *Her dragon!*

"Yes," the voice echoed through his head as if it were picking up his thoughts. *"I was hers. We are bound. You are mine. Save me!"*

"How?" Noah asked the dragon. A flash of knowledge slammed into his head, making him gasp. A spell. Very old and very powerful.

"Free me. Save me!"

Noah nodded as he started to draw the power he would need to work the spell. He now knew what the mages had been trying to do. The spell they had been using was a poorly managed version of the one the dragon had just given him. Placing his hand over the wound in Raven's chest, he poured the power out and chanted the words. He wasn't quite sure what they were, for they were in a language older than most could remember, but he knew what the spell would do. The dragon had shown him.

As the words flowed from him, the air around them shimmered with energy. The power trapped in Raven's lifeless body condensed and crystalized under Noah's fingers. After a few moments of concentration, he held a mass of diamond shards the size of a baseball. He rolled the ball over, careful not to cut himself on the razor-sharp edges. The center of the crystal pulsed with a reddish light. He knew what this was. *A dragon heart.*

Back in the days of old, dragon-heart stones were used to bond mates together. Unlike the sharing of a scale, a heart stone wouldn't just give the mate the life of the dragon. It gave them part of the powers of the dragon. A heart stone was formed, and the bonded pair would use the crystal to divide the dragon's power in half. But the spell was risky. If the human accepting the bond wasn't strong enough in mind, the dragon would take over and run rampant through the country. It also took a powerful dragon to withstand being fractured. As time ran on and the dragons' powers were divided, fewer and fewer dragons could stand the split. The art of sharing a scale came into practice, and heart stones fell out of use and onto the pages of mythology. Noah knew of the archaic custom because he'd come across it in an old text while they were researching Michael's situation, but it had only been mentioned in passing. He'd found other references to heart stones scattered through several old vellum volumes—

warnings of the dangers of the practice, but nothing on how it was done.

Noah stared at the heart in awe. It was beautiful, but he didn't know if it would remain so. *How long can a dragon survive in this form?* He pondered this for a moment, but Raven's dying words echoed through his brain, pushing him to act. Unwilling to risk losing the dragon, he squeezed the gem, slicing the diamond points deep into his palm. Rolling his hand over, he let his blood seep out onto the heart. The power of the dragon raced up his arm, slamming into his brain. A mighty roar shook his world.

"*Mine!*" the dragon roared as it claimed its new home.

Noah fought for control over the beast, but the dragon's rage gave it an unnatural strength. The desire to destroy everything that had hurt Raven coursed through him. "No!" he cried out. Dropping the blood-covered heart, he wrapped his arms around Raven's body, trying to hold on to himself, but the dragon was too strong. It ripped its way out of Noah's body, taking Noah for a ride. The leather collar around his neck forced the dragon into a size smaller than it was used to, but this size was more than enough to do what it wanted for the moment. Noah's consciousness dropped away as the creature pounced on the body of the man who had killed Raven and started ripping it to shreds.

"RAVEN!" Daniel called as he banged on the front door of her home. It was well after two o'clock, and Noah hadn't checked in yet. "*Where is he?*" He jiggled the door handle and found it locked. "If you don't answer in the next ten seconds, we're coming in!" When no answer came, Daniel turned to the men standing behind him and stepped out of the way. "Break it down."

The four men dressed in heavy SWAT outfits hefted the metal battering ram and swung it at the door. It cracked under the pressure. Drawing back the heavy, steel head, they swung it into the wood again. The latch broke loose, and the door banged open.

"Raven!" Daniel yelled as he stormed into the foyer. A feeling of wrongness hit him, stopping him in his tracks. "*Find them!*" he bellowed to the men following him through the door. His team spread out as he headed towards the stairs leading to the living space. Since he had been in Raven's home before, he knew exactly where to look. Noah was most likely being held in Raven's master bedroom.

Slamming into the room, Daniel paused to look around. The smell of dragon pheromones was heavy in the air, but the room held no signs of Raven or Noah.

The radio on Daniel's shoulder crackled to life. "Commander."

Daniel grabbed up the mic and snapped it on. "Did you find him?" Worry had settled into his heart.

"We found something," the man answered back. "You had better come and see this." There was a hint of horror in the man's voice.

"On my way." Clicking the radio into place, Daniel stormed back out of the bedroom, pondering their situations. *What the hell is Raven up to, and where is Noah?*

A small group of men were waiting at the bottom of the steps when Daniel came down. He looked at them expectantly.

One of the men held out his hand and pointed down the hall. "This way, sir."

Daniel nodded and turned down the hall. The strong smell of blood quickened his steps. Fear for Noah's health clawed at Daniel, and he reprimanded himself. He should never have let Noah go with that crazy woman. This could be worse than the last time she had claimed one of his men. At least then, his man had survived the encounter. A group of men stood in the doorway of what he knew was Raven's dining room. "What is it?" he said as he came up and stopped behind them. They filled the doorway, making it impossible to see what was beyond.

One of the men turned around and looked at him. "Sir!" he said as he stepped back from the door.

Daniel looked at the man. His eyes were wide in shock, and he looked rather green. Turning to the room, he pushed his way through the remaining men and stopped as soon as he saw the carnage. It looked like a bomb had gone off.

The beautiful wooden table that Daniel knew had been in there was reduced to splinters. The wallpaper and curtains were rent with claw marks. What looked to be the remains of bodies were shredded all over everything. And right in the middle of the whole mess lay a black dragon glistening with blood.

But the blood and gore wasn't what froze Daniel in his tracks. His eyes barely even noted them. It was the limp form the dragon hunkered down next to that held his attention. He stood there in shock as he studied the scene. He couldn't see the face of the woman who lay untouched in the carnage, but the long strands of dark hair that curled around her body gave Daniel an idea who she was. *Raven.* Dread settled its claws into him. She was much too still to be alive.

Swallowing hard, he turned his attention to the dragon. Its scales were so black they almost shone purple in the light from the broken window. The only dragon he knew with that deep of a color was Raven herself. The dragon was small. Its body was barely the size of a medium dog. The creature practically lay on top of Raven's body, with its face buried in her chest. The glitter of tear-shaped diamonds were scattered over everything.

Daniel brought his hand up to his face and wiped it over his mouth as he took in the horror. The diamond tears of a dragon hurt like hell to cry. The only time he had ever seen a dragon cry was when it lost a mate, and that was usually only one or two. He had never known a dragon to cry this much. Besides, Raven didn't have a mate. Pulling himself together, Daniel stepped into the room.

The dragon's head popped up from where it had been resting on the woman's body. Another tear fell to the floor with a soft click. The creature turned dark eyes towards Daniel and glared.

Daniel froze so as not to startle the dragon. "Hello," he called softly to the creature.

The dragon growled at him and kneaded the floor with its claws. Long strips of wood curled away as the sharp talons rent the polished surface.

Kneeling down, Daniel offered his hand to the dragon. "We're here to help."

The dragon growled again and moved closer to Raven's body. It was clear she had been something special to the creature.

"Tell me who you are," Daniel said, trying to coax the dragon into talking as he inched closer to the pair.

The beast tensed as the distance between them narrowed. Finally, when it felt Daniel was too close, it launched itself at him.

Having practiced this before, Daniel was prepared for the attack and twisted to avoid the creature's powerful jaws. He grabbed it by the front legs and wrenched it around to slam it on the ground next to him. Even though the thing was small, it thrashed violently under him. Two of the men standing in the doorway were on the dragon in a heartbeat. It took all three of them to wrestle the thing to the ground.

The dragon let out a heartbreaking keening as two more men came in to tie the poor thing up.

Daniel sat up and moved away from the struggling pile of men and dragon. Now that the creature was taken care of, he was free to examine the scene. Looking back at the mess in the center of the room, he crept closer to the fallen woman. It was most definitely Raven. Carefully, Daniel rolled her over. The front of her dress was soaked in blood, but it wasn't hard to find the hole in her chest where the knife had punctured her heart. "Oh, Raven," he said softly as he caressed the hair back from her face. "What happened here?" he asked.

His only answer was a high-pitched wail from the dragon.

Daniel turned to look at the thing still struggling under the men. They were doing their best to hold it down until the medical team could get there with sedatives to calm it. As he turned back to Raven's body, Daniel's eye caught on something unusual next to her. He reached out to get the strange item and stopped as soon as his fingers touched it. Pain raced through him as the residual energy slammed into his mind, washing it with the recent memories of the dragon. They ripped through his brain, setting off a seizure that dropped him to the floor thrashing.

When Daniel regained his senses, he was stretched out on the floor of the foyer with a medic standing over him. "The dragon?" he gasped as the sound of his own voice echoed through his head, making it ache.

"It's all right," the medic soothed him, "it's been sedated." The man nodded to a lump on the far side of the room.

Daniel waved the man away and rolled off the mat the medic had laid him on. "Get me Laurence," he said as he pushed the blanket off.

The EMT's hands came up and caught Daniel on the shoulders, stopping him from getting up. "Sir, you need to rest. An ambulance is on the way."

"I don't need an ambulance," Daniel growled, "I need Laurence!" He shoved the man back and forced his way up from the ground. "*Laurence!*"

"Yes, sir," Laurence answered as he loped into the room.

Daniel waved to him. "Come here." When the larger man stepped close, Daniel grabbed him and staggered across the room to the dragon. He paused as he looked over the cloth-wrapped creature. The poor thing was out cold. Dropping to his knees next to the beast, Daniel tugged on the cloth, loosening the small animal's bindings. "I'm sorry." A tear ran down his cheek as the dragon's memories raced through his head. He searched the dragon for injuries. There were a few spots that were roughed up, but it looked to be in good health. He also noted a black leather band wrapped high around the creatures throat, but the clasp was up under the boney frill and would require some work to get off. He decided to leave it for later. Once he was sure the dragon was fine, he ran his fingers over the boned frill at the back of its head. "I'll get the king, and we will figure this out."

Patting the warm scales one last time, he turned to look up at Laurence. "Grab four men and take this dragon back to the main office. Get him secured in one of the guest rooms and see that a medic checks him over. I want to make sure we didn't hurt him."

"Yes, sir," Laurence said as he nodded. Reaching down, he helped Daniel from the floor.

Once Daniel was on his feet again, he patted Laurence on the arm. "And stay with him." He nodded down at the small dragon. "He's going to need someone familiar nearby when he wakes up."

Laurence gave Daniel a confused look. "Yes, sir," he agreed.

Daniel nodded once more and stepped away to stand on his own. There was much he needed to do, and he didn't know how long he had to do it. First, he needed to find something to collect that sphere before anyone else touched it and figured out what it was. Then, he had to find a place to hide it away until he could figure out what to do with it. Only then could he take the whole mess to Kyle. Maybe he would know what to do.

"Daniel," Laurence called before his boss could get out of the room.

Daniel paused and looked back at him with a raised eyebrow.

"Who is it?" Laurence glanced down at the sleeping dragon.

The corner of Daniel's mouth turned up in amusement. *Of course he hasn't figured it out.* "It's Noah."

Laurence's mouth dropped open in shock, and he turned wide eyes to the small pile of dragon.

A smile turned up the rest of Daniel's lips. If the situation hadn't been so serious, the look on the normally unflappable man's face would have made his day.

Chapter 3

The rain beat down on the pavement as Kara sat in her borrowed car and stared out at the main building of Eternity. This was just not her day. Grumbling, she reached for the umbrella she always kept under the seat but came up empty-handed. *Crap.* Letting out a sigh, she leaned her head forwards onto the steering wheel and resisted the urge to scream. Of course the umbrella was not there. It was under *her* seat in *her* car back at the shop, where they were putting a new head on the engine. Grabbing her attaché, she shoved the door open, climbed out into the light rain, and raised the case over her head in a vain attempt to keep dry. She wasn't even supposed to be here today.

Today was supposed to have been dedicated to organizing her new home. She had spent yesterday moving her things into a nice townhouse just minutes from her new office across town. Most of the furniture was in place, and the large boxes had been moved into the proper rooms. Now all Kara had to do was sort through the small things and make the space her own. She had been elbow-deep in packing peanuts when Daniel called, demanding that she come into the main office for an emergency. *An emergency!* She was a therapist, for goodness sakes. The only thing close to an emergency she'd ever seen was a dragon that couldn't shift, and that was more of an inconvenience. In those cases, the dragon king was called in directly to suppress the out-of-control dragon and help them shift back to human. She dealt with the individuals afterwards to help them work through their issues. She couldn't think of *anything* she could do that couldn't wait until Monday. When she'd told Daniel this, he threated to throw her in the brig for insubordination and have her court-martialed! That had gotten Kara up and moving fast. Never in the years she'd worked in Eternity had anyone *ever* pulled rank on her.

After checking for traffic, Kara loped across the road, hoping to make it into the main building before the weather completely drenched her lovely, new suit. The call from Daniel had her so flustered that she hadn't even considered a rain jacket when she'd left home. She glanced up at the sky as she reached the curb. The clouds looked horrible, but the rain was starting to let up. Dropping her case to her side, she hurried along the sidewalk. She could move faster if she weren't supporting that thing on her head.

Kara's flight was interrupted just feet from her goal when her foot came down and her heel sunk in further than it should have. The unexpected drop, coupled with her speed, was a fatal combination. She threw her arms out to catch her balance but failed. With a loud crack, gravity won out, and she ended up sprawled across the sidewalk in a puddle. Kara lay on the sidewalk for a moment, breathing past the pain in her knee and resisting the growing urge to scream. It was so tempting to thrash about and let out the tantrum building inside her, but she took several deep breaths before pulling herself up to inspect the damage she'd done.

Her physical injuries weren't bad. The heels of both her hands were a little raw, but not really cut up. She did have a bit of road rash on her knee, but that was nominal compared to the damage she had done to her outfit. She might be able to save the light blue pencil skirt and matching jacket from the dirty water she had fallen into, but her shoes were a total loss. The spindly heel had come down in the soft caulking in the sidewalk and had broken clean off the body of the shoe. Kara glared at the damaged heel sticking out of the sidewalk mocking her.

"Are you all right, Miss Rose?"

Kara looked up as the light rain stopped. A large man dressed in a black Eternity uniform stood over her with an umbrella. It took her a moment to register the man's words. He had used her name. She had no idea who he was, but he had obviously been told to watch out for her. There was no other reason he would know her name. She hadn't been to the main office in a while. And of course she would make the most embarrassing entrance possible. She ran her hand down her skirt, hoping it hadn't slipped up far enough to show anything off.

Letting out a deep sigh, she shook her head in disbelief. *Could this day get any worse?* "I'm fine," she answered, taking the hand the man offered to get up. "It's just been one of those days."

The man chuckled softly as he reached down and picked up her briefcase. "I know what you mean." He held the bag out to her.

Bending at the waist, Kara ripped what was left of her heel from the sidewalk and kicked out of her shoes. At this point, there was no reason to even try to be professional.

Hopefully, someone inside would have an extra uniform she could borrow for a while. Grabbing up her ruined shoes, she turned to the guard holding her bag. "Thank you."

A warm smile slipped across his face. "You're welcome."

Kara considered him for a moment. His pearly white teeth shone brightly against his dark skin. He was also much heavier in size than most of the guards of Eternity. He would probably be very impressive in his grand dragon form. But, then again, you couldn't really tell much about a person's dragon from their human form. Some of the largest dragons she had ever met were rather small people. Kara shook her thoughts away and smiled back at the man. "Are you here to meet me?"

His grin widened. "Yes. Daniel asked that I show you directly to him. Call me Mac."

"Thank you, Mac." Kara slipped her ruined shoes into her bag and settled her things back into place. Once she was done, she looked back up at Mac. "Whenever you're ready."

Mac chuckled and held out his hand towards a part in the fence. "This way."

Kara started off, and Mac fell into step next to her, holding the umbrella between them. "So…" she shot the man a sidelong look, "what's the emergency?"

The happy look on Mac's face dropped, leaving a level of seriousness that worried Kara. "I think it's best if you talk to Daniel about that."

Concerned by his words, Kara gave him a surprised look before letting the conversation drop and turning her attention back to where they were going. *What could this emergency be?* She was a counselor that specialized in a very narrow field of mental health. Give her a disconnected dragon, and she could work wonders. Give her anything else, and she was almost as clueless as a monkey doing math.

Kara turned possible scenarios over in her mind as Mac led her through the halls of the main office. Even though it had been a while since she'd been there, she knew her way around pretty well. She paused for a heartbeat when Mac passed up the turn leading to Daniel's office and headed down the hall to the holding cells. Her brow creased in confusion when they came upon a group of men standing outside one of the cells.

It wasn't uncommon to see groups of soldiers standing around waiting on something, but these looked like they had been on the losing end of some epic battle. They were rumpled and torn up. A few sported bleeding bites, and one was holding a bag of ice to what looked to be a burn. The group huddled together, peeking through a small window in a door.

Mac stopped a few paces back from them and held out his hand, ushering Kara on.

Kara glanced at him before walking past and up to the men. Each one stepped back and let her closer to the small window. The looks on their faces frightened her. She turned towards the glass, not knowing if she wanted to see what was inside. Gathering her courage, she stepped up and looked through the window.

The room beyond was fairly small. Nothing really remarkable about it. Just a simple holding cell with a concrete bed on one side and a metal toilet on the other. What was remarkable was the condition it was in. The metal toilet had been ripped from the floor, and water sprayed out over the torn-up shreds of what was left of the pad that had been on the bench. There were long claw marks down the walls. They hadn't really damaged the brick walls, but the paint job was toasted. And speaking of toasted, there were huge soot stains on the walls where something had tried to set them on fire. Right in the middle of the whole mess was the culprit. A small, black dragon, no larger than a dog. It stared at the door as if it were daring someone to open it. As Kara met its eyes, a trickle of smoke rolled out of the beast's nose, and it growled. The thing launched itself at the window.

Kara jumped back as the creature slammed into the heavy glass. Hands of the men around her caught her before she could hit the ground again. As she regained her balance, she listened to the dragon terrorize the cell. Never in her time as a counselor had she seen a dragon lose it like that. A sinking feeling settled into the pit of her stomach as she stared at the door to the cell. *Is this the reason Daniel called?*

"Did you see him?"

Whipping around, Kara found the owner of the voice. Daniel and two more men, both looking worse for wear, had just turned into the cell block.

Kara pointed a shaking hand at the door. "Is that why you called me?"

Daniel passed her up and went to look in through the window. The door rattled as the small dragon slammed into it again. "Unfortunately, yes." He sighed, turning to look at Kara. "He needs help."

Easing her way up to the window again, she watched as the dragon ripped into a large chunk of bedding and shook it violently. *No fucking way!* "I think you had better call Kyle or Carissa for this one," she said as she stepped back from the window before the dragon saw her and attacked the door again. "This is way above me."

A forlorn look came over Daniel's face, and he stared at her for a moment before looking in the window. "The king and Carissa have both been by. They were unable to help. He's gone feral."

Feral! Kara's heart clenched. For a dragon to go feral, their two halves would have to be completely separated. It wasn't an uncommon thing in the old days, but in today's world, the signs of distress were well-known. Someone should have noticed long before the dragon had lost control. Kara peeked back into the room. This dragon had either suffered in silence for a long time or experienced an intensely traumatic event.

Daniel pulled in a long breath and pushed away from the door, drawing Kara's attention from the dragon. "Besides, Kyle doesn't have the time to work on this right now. He's going to have his hands full this afternoon when he announces the murder of an Ancient."

"An Ancient!" Shock colored Kara's voice. Very old dragons were treasured. For someone to kill one was unheard of. "Who?"

"Raven Nightingale."

Kara stood in disbelief. Raven was one of the most distinguished dragons around. Even though she was a recluse, her reach was vast. Everyone knew who she was. Announcing her murder was going to rock the dragon world. "Who did it?"

Daniel shrugged. "Don't know." He looked up at the door. "Noah in there is the only living witness."

Pushing her hands up over her damp hair, Kara tried to get herself together. The death of Raven was shocking, and to have the only witness go feral was bad beyond words. No wonder Daniel had insisted she come as fast as she could. She turned the situation over in her mind, trying to figure out how she could help. Once she had gotten her thoughts straight, she turned back to Daniel. "Tell me what happened."

KARA STOOD in front of the cell door and contemplated her course of action. The tale Daniel had spun was preposterous, yet his men had backed him up one hundred percent. It was hard to believe the dragon beyond the door had been a human just a few days ago, but Daniel had explained it and shown her the heart stone responsible for transferring the dragon. Kara had never heard of that form of sharing a dragon, but Daniel had assured her it was real, and he would know. He wasn't as old as some of the Ancients, but he was older than most of the dragons she knew.

But that didn't matter. What *did* matter was that she had a person whose human and dragon parts were completely separate. This she understood and could work with. She had never seen a case as severe as this, but the concepts needed to reunite the pieces were the same. Marrying two halves that had never been one was the part that worried Kara the most.

Taking a deep breath, Kara took a step towards the door.

"Are you sure you want to go in there like that?"

Pausing, Kara looked at the tall man next to her and studied him for a moment. Of all the men in the hall, Laurence was sporting the deepest bites and wounds from the small dragon. He was also supposed to be Noah's closest friend. In fact, all the men were people Noah was supposed to know, but the little dragon had attacked them all without mercy. An offhanded tease by one of the men had made her second-guess changing into the clean uniform Daniel had found for her. If Noah and the dragon weren't connected, the dragon might not recognize the men as friends. It might just see the uniform and recall the men who had captured and drugged it. If she put on that same uniform, there was a good chance it would lump her in with the people the dragon saw as the enemy. Since her outfit was mostly ruined anyway, she thought it was worth risking its complete destruction verses the bites and burns she was sure to get in the Eternity uniform.

"Yes, Laurence, I'm sure." She bent over and snagged the broken shoe out of her bag, just in case. "Let's do this."

Laurence shrugged, unlatched the door, and pulled it open just enough for her to slip in.

The sound of the bolt sliding home unnerved Kara, but she kept her eyes trained on the small dragon hunkered down in the center of the room. It watched her closely as she stood there, taking the scene in. The room was more trashed than she'd been able to see from the outside. Blood and soot stained everything. Chunks of concrete were missing from the bed, and the metal toilet was shredded beyond recognition. Thankfully, Daniel had had someone turn off the water so it wasn't fountaining anymore, but everything was still soaked.

Once she was sure of her surroundings, Kara focused solely on the dragon. The fact that it hadn't immediately attacked her when she had come in made her glad she hadn't changed into the Eternity uniform. "Hello," she said softly.

The dragon dropped into a protective stance and pulled its wings in tight against its body.

Kara watched his body language very closely as she took her first slow step into the room. "I'm not here to hurt you."

Letting out a soft growl, the dragon's back end wiggled like a cat getting ready to pounce.

"My name is Kara, and I just want to talk." She spoke softly as she continued into the room.

After two more small steps, the dragon attacked, but Kara was ready for him. Raising the shoe, she bashed him in the side of the head, knocking his sharp teeth away. Once he was off balance, she grabbed the edge of the crest at the back of his head and twisted it over so he landed on his back with a yelp of surprise. Taking full advantage of his astonishment, she spun him around so his head was towards her and dropped down on his nose so her knee held his mouth shut in case he decided to bite. Leaning her full weight on his frill, she pinned him to the floor. One eye, wide with surprise, stared up at her as they came to rest on the floor together.

"Enough of this!" she snapped as the dragon flailed. When his sharp claws got near her, she swatted them away again. "*Enough!*" Taking the shoe, she smacked him hard in the chest, knocking the wind from him. When he gasped, she dropped the shoe and bent her forehead to the bottom of his chin. She rubbed against him as he panted for breath.

It was a dirty trick, using a courtship gesture in his time of distress, but she needed him calm and it was one of the few things she knew that would take the fight out of a worked-up dragon. She drew in a long breath from his skin as she rubbed her cheek and face against him. A whole mess of scent hit her, making her reel. *No wonder he's attacking everything. He's so far out of balance it's amazing he's conscious at all.* Shaking her thoughts away, she continued to nuzzle him until the tension in his muscles eased.

Once he was calm, Kara sat up and looked at him. He was beautiful—or he would be, once he was cleaned up. The spray from the broken toilet had done some good, removing part of the dirt and blood coating his scales, but he was in desperate need of a real bath. There was some form of band around his neck, but she would have to get closer to inspect it fully. That could wait until later.

He lay there, limp under her steady hold. The tip of his tail flipping back and forth was the only suggestion he might still be upset. "If I turn you lose, will you behave yourself?"

The dragon rumbled softly.

"Words," Kara insisted. "You have them, use them. I will understand."

It took the dragon a moment, but it rumbled a very guttural yes.

"Very well." Slowly, Kara eased off the dragon's chin and frill.

It lay there for a moment before carefully rolling over, catching Kara in one big, glassy eye to study her.

"I'm sorry about that," Kara said as she shifted around to sit more comfortably on the damp floor. She tugged at her skirt, trying to get it into a more decent position. When she saw it wasn't going to go, she gave up and turned her attention fully to her new patient. "You want to try this again from the beginning?" she asked, giving him a soft smile.

The dragon just stared at her.

Amusement curled up the corner of her mouth, and she let out a soft laugh. "Well, I think we should." She cleared her throat, trying to make herself seem more professional. "My name is Kara Rose, and Daniel called me to come help. I'm a counselor."

A doubtful look crossed the dragon's face.

Kara smiled at him. "I'm not going to claim to know what you've been through or try to understand your situation." She paused and studied the dragon for a moment before continuing. "Daniel has given me an idea of what happened, and I don't think anyone could really understand what you've gone through. But I'm here to help you connect with your human half."

The dragon rumbled softly.

Kara snickered in reply. "Well, I'm here to help you connect with Noah."

"Mine!" the dragon growled and recoiled from her.

"Easy there," Kara said as she held out her hands, trying to soothe the beast. "No one's going to take him away from you."

The dragon relaxed back into his resting position.

"Noah's got a lot of friends who are worried about him. They just want to make sure he's all right," Kara explained. She considered the dragon's posture for a moment. He was relaxed and showing no signs of the aggression he'd had a few moments ago. That was a good sign. "He *is* all right, isn't he?"

The dragon blinked but didn't answer.

A note of dread crept into Kara's heart. She didn't like the fact that the dragon couldn't tell her if Noah was okay. "Can I speak with him?"

Pain colored the dragon's dark eyes. "Lost!" it moaned and rolled its head away from Kara.

The note of despair in the creature's voice broke Kara's heart. She shifted over so she was right next to his head. "Come here." She pulled his head into her lap. "If Noah were truly lost, you wouldn't be here." She ran her fingers over his warm scales, comforting him. "It's a proven fact that it takes two parts for a dragon to survive. He's in there—we just have to find him."

The dragon blinked, considering her words. "Truly?"

"Truly," Kara answered back. "And we *will* find him. Together."

The dragon rolled his head over and pressed it into her middle.

Letting out a sigh, Kara held his head. Usually, she didn't let her patients get this physical, but this was by far the worst case of separation she had ever seen. Normally, it only took a little convincing to get the dragon to back down and let the human half out. She had never seen a case where the dragon couldn't reach their other side at all.

"Scared," he rumbled.

Kara squeezed him tighter. "It will be all right," she soothed him. After a moment, she released him and pushed him back so she could look in his face. "But first we have to figure out what to call you. You aren't Raven anymore, and you aren't Noah." She paused as she thought about it. "What would you like to be called?"

The dragon blinked at her, unsure.

After a moment of indecision, Kara smiled at him. "Why don't we call you Byrd, since Raven's last name was Nightingale and Noah's last name is Dove? Sound good?"

The dragon snickered and nodded its head. "Byrd," he chirped.

"All right, Byrd. What say you and I blow this popsicle stand and go find something to eat?" Kara suggested. "I don't know about you, but I could really use a good steak about now."

Byrd nodded again and moved back so Kara could get up.

Pushing up from the floor, Kara straightened out her suit and looked down at her new patient. His wings hung low under the weight of his situation. Letting out a deep sigh, Kara shifted over and rubbed her fingers over Byrd's shoulders.

The little dragon leaned into her side, accepting her touch.

She scratched a little harder as they turned towards the door.

Laurence eyed the quiet dragon but opened the door leading to the hall where the rest of the men were waiting.

Byrd growled softly until Kara patted him on the back.

"These men are your friends," she reminded him.

He quieted down but watched the men warily as she guided him out of the room.

Daniel stood against the far wall with a smile on his face. "That was surprisingly easy. So when can I have my man back?"

Kara laughed. He had no idea the scale of the task they had in front of them. And it was going to be hell if facing down a feral dragon with a broken shoe was the *easy* part.

THE EBB and flow of a heated conversation was the first thing Noah recognized as he floated on the edge of awareness. Memories toyed with his brain, but he couldn't quite grasp them. Something significant had happened, but he couldn't recall what it had been. He didn't really hurt, just felt a little disconnected from his body. Like that time when he'd been playing with a volatile spell and had ended up in the hospital for a week. The out-of-body experience that had caused was very similar to how he felt now, but this was the other way around. Instead of being trapped outside his body looking down, he was stuck inside looking out with someone else in control.

He listened to the conversation, not really understanding what the voices were saying. From the timber, he could tell it was a male and a female talking passionately about something. But what eluded him.

As they went on, Noah slowly caught the gist of their argument. The girl wanted to do something, and the guy was refusing. The male's voice was familiar, and Noah raised his head to look at the man. The world looked weird. Colors were overly bright, and the edges of everything were too sharp. He blinked a few times, trying to focus on the man. It took Noah a moment to identify him. *Daniel.* Noah looked over at the animated woman arguing with him. She was a mess. Her long hair hung loose around her shoulders in damp tendrils, and her well-cut suit was smudged with dirt and soaked beyond repair. Noah stared at the pair, wondering why they were arguing.

"She wants us to go with her."

Noah looked around for the source of the new voice but couldn't find anyone else. He tried to call out to ask, but nothing came out. "*Who?*" he asked in his head.

A soft snicker washed over him. "*We are one.*"

Noah paused as he recognized the voice. "*Dragon?*"

The dragon rumbled in response.

Noah felt the unusual sensation vibrate up from his own chest. The argument between Daniel and the woman paused in response to the sound.

"How about we ask him?" she snapped at Daniel.

Daniel looked at the woman, considering her request. "Sure." He turned his attention to Noah. "Byrd, if I let you go with Miss Rose, will you behave and work to get my man back to me?"

Noah wanted to answer him, to tell Daniel he was there, but the dragon took control.

"Yes, we be good," it chirped.

Daniel considered him. "And Noah?"

"We find him," Byrd answered.

Noah wanted to scream. He pushed and pulled with all his might, but nothing he did made a difference. He was stuck at the mercy of the dragon, forced to watch as the woman turned back to Daniel.

"See, he'll behave," she argued. "I'll make sure he's all right." She paused as Daniel mulled over the decision. "He isn't doing you any good as he is, and I can't help him here. He needs a quiet place to recover, not a cell."

Daniel let out a frustrated sigh. "Fine. Take him. Keep him with you at all times. He's your responsibility and top priority. I want him back safe and whole as soon as possible. Do I make myself clear?"

The woman looked ready to snap at Daniel, but she clenched her teeth and nodded. "Crystal." Without another word, she turned from Daniel to face Noah. There was a hint of irritation in her eyes, but she smiled warmly at him. "Come on, sweetheart, let's get out of here."

Noah felt his head nod as the dragon agreed. "*We're going to go with her?*" he questioned. A hint of fear echoed through him. The last time he had gone with a woman he didn't know, it hadn't ended well.

"She's nice," the dragon answered as he turned and followed the woman out.

If it had been possible, Noah would have let out a deep sigh of frustration as he sat back and hung on for the ride. It was weird not being in control of his body.

Chapter 4

Sitting in her driveway, Kara stared out the front window of her car at her house. *I can't believe I'm doing this!* As a therapist, she lived by two rules: never get physical with your patients, and never bring them into your personal life. Two very important boundaries when dealing with creatures that put a lot more emphasis on physical touch and personal space than humans did.

It was never a good idea to put yourself into a situation where an emotionally distressed dragon might start to depend on you. That was the way unintentional bonds were formed. Such situations usually ended badly. Kara had broken her physical contact rule on occasions when her patients needed that extra support, but she never let it go too far.

The second rule had *never* been broken. She refused to cross the line between professional and personal for any reason. Yet, here she was, sitting in her driveway with the most distressed dragon she had ever met—one she'd already broken her first rule with—getting ready to break her most sacred, second rule.

She glanced over at the small dragon next to her. He looked so forlorn with his chin up on the dashboard, staring out the windshield at her home. The sight softened her resistance and made the corner of her mouth turn up in a gentle smile. "Come on," she said as she gathered up her things and got out of the car, holding the door open for the little dragon.

Byrd blinked up at her for a moment before climbing across the seats and out her side of the car.

"Please excuse the mess," Kara said as she led the way to the house and unlocked the door. "I'm still in the process of moving in." She pushed the door wide for Byrd to pass.

Byrd stopped on the threshold and glanced up at her as if he were unsure about entering her home.

"Go on," she urged. "Daniel said you have to stay with me for a while."

After another long moment of slow blinks, Byrd nodded his head and slipped through the door.

Kara let out a long sigh. *So much for rules.* Shaking off her irritation, she followed Byrd through the door and nearly ran over him. He'd stopped just inside the living room and was staring at the row of boxes piled against the wall. "I told you it was a mess," she said as she shifted past him and dropped her things on the end of the couch. "I actually just moved in yesterday." She turned and looked at the pensive dragon. "Come on and I'll show you around."

Byrd nodded and followed her.

"This is the living room." She held her hand out to show off the room before stepping into the connected kitchen. "And the kitchen." This room was also stacked with boxes. "I'm a pretty good cook, but we'll have to order out until I get my dishes unpacked." She pointed to an area stacked with more boxes. "The table will be over here eventually." She smiled back at Byrd. "I haven't picked it out yet."

The dragon nodded again.

"This place is bigger than my last apartment," she explained as she led the way out of the kitchen to a narrow set of stairs. "I was so excited to find it at such an amazing steal." Kara rambled on as she led the way up to the second floor. "There's a half bath downstairs, but the bedrooms are up here." Pushing open the first door, she showed off a room stuffed with boxes. "Here's the library—or will be, when I get it sorted." Continuing down the hall, she led him to another door. "This is my office and the guest room." Holding the door open, she let him go in.

After a few steps into the room, Byrd stopped and glanced around.

The way he sat back on his haunches and wrapped his tail around his feet irritated Kara. She looked around the modest room. On one wall were her desk and the filing cabinets holding her work. On the other wall was a perfectly nice daybed. The mattress, however, was leaned against the wall, and the pillows were still in plastic. Kara let out a sigh. At least the white iron frame had been put together. Forcing a smile on her face, she turned to the little dragon. "I'm sorry. I wasn't expecting company so soon. If you give me five minutes to get cleaned up, I'll get this made up for you."

Biting back the anger riding her, she turned and left the little dragon alone. Pushing into her room, she ripped the ruined shirt off and threw it on the floor. This whole day was getting to her. Stopping in front of her closet, she closed her eyes and drew in a deep, calming breath. She had to get a handle on herself before she snapped and said something she would regret. It wasn't Byrd's fault he was here. She needed him to trust her so she could help him.

Snapping at him would only put space between them and delay her ability to sort him out.

Opening her eyes, she looked into the closet to find something suitable to wear. Pulling out jeans and a T-shirt, she grabbed some clean underwear from a box and took them into her bathroom to change. A quick glance in the mirror made her change her mind about her course of action. She had planned on just washing her face and changing clothes, but she was more of a mess than she'd realized. Dropping her clothing on the counter, she turned and cranked on the water. It would have to be a fast shower, but there was no way she was going to deal with clean linens when she was covered in mud and soot. Stripping the rest of the way out of her clothing, she stepped into the water. Being clean would go a long way towards settling her world down so she could work.

NOAH LOOKED around the room Kara had left him in.

"*Looks nice*," he told Byrd. He could feel the dragon's reluctance to agree. "*Now don't be snobby,*" he warned, "*she wasn't expecting guests. There's a lot of potential here.*"

Byrd shrugged and got up to investigate the room. Together, they poked through some of the boxes. A few held pillows and linens that Noah thought would look nice on the iron daybed. Others held books or knickknacks. A well-executed picture of some English countryside leaned against the wall opposite the undressed window.

Noah nodded his approval. "*This place will look splendid once she gets it put together.*"

Byrd shrugged again.

Noah would have let out a deep sigh if he could have.

Heading for the door, Byrd stuck his head out into the

hall. He could hear water running from the end of the hall Kara hadn't shown them. Following the sound, he stuck his head into an open door. There was a large bed against one wall and more boxes piled around.

"I think this is her room," Noah warned. He could feel the dragon's curiosity pique as they moved into the room. "*We should probably leave her be while she's changing.*"

Byrd snorted, ignoring Noah, and slipped into the room. He poked around for a moment before going over and pressing his nose against the unlatched bathroom door. It started to inch open.

"No, Byrd!" Noah argued, forcing his will out, trying to take control away from the dragon.

Byrd stopped and shook his head as if he were trying to silence Noah.

"Leave her be," Noah coaxed. "*She's having a rough day already.*" He didn't need to know all of her story to see she was having a hard time. The fight with Daniel and the condition of her clothing were more than enough to prove that.

"Make better," Byrd argued and nosed the door again.

Noah clench down as hard as he could on the muscles in his legs, and they stopped moving forwards. "*No, Byrd.*"

Byrd shook himself again.

"We can make her day better by letting her have some time to regroup," Noah coaxed the dragon. He could feel the creature's indecision. Byrd wanted to go in and comfort her, but he was starting to see Noah's point. "*Just let her be for a little while.*"

Shaking himself again, Byrd backed away from the open door. *Explore.* Turning, he made his way out of Kara's room and back down the hall.

Noah breathed a sigh of relief as they made their way

down the hall. He wasn't sure what Kara would have done had they barged in on her shower.

"Why?" Byrd asked, picking up on Noah's thoughts.

"You know, for an old dragon, you sure are naive about things," Noah complained, but the question hung between them. Letting out another sigh, he explained, *"People like privacy when showering or changing. It makes them uncomfortable when others watch while they're undressed."*

Byrd thought on this for a moment. *"But Raven not uncomfortable when you watched."*

"That was different," Noah said meekly.

"How?"

"You were there, you know." The dragon's curiosity ate at Noah, and he drew in a frustrated breath as he tried to think of a way to explain it to Byrd. *"We were in a physical relationship. She expected me to watch her undress."*

After a few moments of thought, Byrd paused on the stairs and asked a question that blew Noah's mind. *"Relationship with Kara?"*

"No!" Noah said, stopping the dragon from turning around and going back up the steps. *"We are not in a relationship with Kara!"*

"Could be," Byrd replied.

For one quick moment, Noah shared the memories of Kara holding him down and rubbing her face against the bottom of his jaw. Desire raced through him, pulling a shiver in its wake. He gasped at the powerful response his body had to the memory. *"No,"* he panted as he tried to focus on the here and now. So many times, he had teased his dragon coworkers when their instincts had kicked in and they'd made a fool of themselves. Now he understood their claims that they couldn't help themselves. He had never expected the call of instinct to be so powerful.

"Sure?" Byrd asked, letting the memory of her touch torture Noah.

"I'm sure." Noah gasped as the feeling subsided. He drew in a few deep breaths before they continued down the stairs to explore the rest of Kara's home. Relaxing, Noah thought as he let Byrd poke around in the woman's boxes. He didn't know how, but the dragon was shielding him from those feelings. If, for some reason, Byrd decided to give in to that call, Noah would be unable to do a thing about it.

"SORRY ABOUT THAT," Kara said, shaking her damp hair back and stepping into the room where she'd left Byrd. She had taken a little longer in the shower than she had intended, but she felt much better now that she was clean and dry again. Pausing, she glanced around. "Byrd?" The little dragon was nowhere to be seen.

Shaking her head, Kara turned out of the room. *Of course he isn't here. He's got a whole house to explore,* she thought, scolding herself as she went to find the little dragon. "Byrd," she called as she glanced in rooms as she passed. He wasn't upstairs. "Where are you?"

A strange thumping noise had her hurrying downstairs.

"Byrd?" She paused at the bottom of the steps, but she didn't see him in the living room.

A distressed cry from the kitchen had Kara rushing around the end of the bar. What she found stopped her dead in her tracks, and she covered her mouth in shock. The kitchen was wrecked. Several boxes were knocked over and spilled. Cans and packages of food were scattered all over her new laminate floor, and Byrd stumbled around in the middle of the mess with a box stuck on his head, keening in distress.

Trying to suppress her laughter, she rushed over to him. "Sweetheart," she cooed as she dodged around his flailing wings and caught him by the shoulders.

He chirped in alarm and froze.

"It's all right," she reassured as she pushed the mess out of the way and sat on the floor next to him.

Byrd shook his head, trying to get the box loose, but it was stuck.

Kara ran her hands over his warm scales, calming him. "Easy there." She slipped her hand inside the box and pushed back the flap of cardboard that had gotten stuck on the boned frill at the back of his head. Lifting it up, she pulled the box off.

Byrd snorted and shook his head as he backed away, glaring at the box furiously.

Kara tried to hide her smile, but the cross dragon was just too cute. A soft snicker slipped out, and he turned his angry look to her. "I'm sorry," she apologized, but she couldn't get the grin to go away.

Byrd shot her a hurt look.

Feeling bad about laughing, Kara apologized again. "I'm sorry, Byrd." She set the box to the side and looked around at the mess. "What were you doing?"

"Hungry," Byrd whined. He lowered his head as if he had done something wrong.

Kara's heart broke, and she shifted up so she could catch the dragon around the head and pull him into her chest. "I'm sorry, sweetheart," she said as she held him. "I forgot about food." Letting out a sigh, she dropped back so she could look at her small houseguest. "How about we order a couple of pizzas?"

Byrd considered her for a moment before nodding his head.

Pushing up from the floor, Kara went to get her phone from her bag. "What would you like on it?" she asked.

When Byrd didn't answer, she turned to look at him. He had followed her out of the kitchen but had only gotten as far as the carpeted floor of the dining room before sitting down. Kara watched him, concerned by his posture. He was sitting back on his haunches with his head down and wings drooping loose as if he were depressed, but he was gurgling and chirping to himself. She caught snippets of words but couldn't understand what he was saying.

Her chest tightened as hope filled her. *Could he be talking to Noah?* Unwilling to interrupt his inner dialogue, Kara searched her phone for the closest pizza place and ordered a variety of pizzas. Hopefully, Byrd would like something she ordered.

After a few more minutes of waiting for the dragon to finish whatever conversation he was having—hopefully with Noah—Kara called out to him. "Would you like to come help me put that room together while we wait for food?"

Byrd's head snapped up at the sound of her words. He blinked a few times before chirping his agreement.

"Come on," Kara said as she led the way to the steps. A positive feeling grew in her chest as he followed behind her, still rumbling to himself. If Byrd was talking with Noah already, then maybe there was hope for them yet.

"I TOLD *you to stay out of that box,"* Noah reprimanded Byrd as they followed Kara out of the kitchen

The little dragon plopped down on the carpet just outside the door. "*Hungry.*"

Noah drew in a mental sigh and calmed himself. "*I know you're hungry. I'm hungry, too, but digging in other people's things isn't nice.*"

"*But I likes the squishy, fruity things,*" Byrd whined.

"*I like gummy bears, too,*" Noah soothed him, "*but we should have asked before we got into them.*"

"*Why?*" Byrd whined again.

"*Because they were Kara's.*"

"*But they yummy and I hungry.*"

"*But you can't just take someone else's stuff,*" Noah tried to explain.

"*Why not?*"

The absolute innocence of that question floored Noah. "*For an old dragon, you're pretty ignorant,*" he snapped.

Anger washed over Byrd, and he flooded Noah's mind with information. "*Not dumb!*"

Noah reeled from the sheer amount of knowledge Byrd dumped on him. After a moment, he found his equilibrium and addressed the upset dragon. "*I didn't say you were dumb. I said you were ignorant, and there's a difference. You're not stupid; you're naive in the way the world works.*" This seemed to calm Byrd, so Noah went on. "*How is it that you know so much yet understand so little?*"

Byrd sat quietly, brooding over the question.

Noah pushed him a little. "*Did you ever think that Kara would be upset if we got into her stuff?*"

"*No,*" Byrd grumbled.

"*Do you think we should ask next time?*" Noah asked softly.

"*Raven not let me do anything, either!*" Byrd snapped.

The epiphany hit Noah like a frying pan to the face. It wasn't that Byrd had lived a long time without learning social skills. He hadn't needed them! Raven had been his moral compass. She, as a rational, thinking being, had been able to tell right from wrong and pick the actions that fit within social standards. Byrd, without that rational thinking, was driven by instinct and desire alone. If he wanted something, he didn't see any reason not to just take it. Noah pondered this, rearranging his views on dragon kind. With everything he knew of dragons, this view made perfect sense. Two entities sharing a body. Both highly intelligent. One rational. One instinctual. It explained so much randomness that he'd seen and dealt with. It also gave him some idea of what he needed to do to regain some control over his life and body.

"*Byrd,*" Noah soothed the irritated dragon, "*this is new to us both, but please, let me help you through it.*"

Byrd grumbled at him.

"Byrd," Kara called out to him.

Byrd's head popped up to look at her.

"Would you like to come help me put that room together while we wait for food?"

A wave of emotion washed over Noah as Byrd stared at Kara. The mix was hard for Noah to name, but he did recognize something. Desire. It wasn't so much the lustful feeling that had come with Byrd's memories. It was more of a need to please Kara.

Noah jumped on it when he felt Byrd's reluctance to do work. "*Why don't we help her?*" he pushed.

Byrd paused before answering him.

Noah could feel the argument rising in the dragon. Byrd was still hungry and didn't like the idea of working on an empty stomach. But Noah knew the dragon was drawn to the woman. "*It would make Kara happy,*" he coaxed.

Byrd gave in to Noah's persuasion and chirped his agreement to Kara.

Noah let out a sigh as Kara led them upstairs to get to

work. Byrd still had control over what they did, but he was starting to understand what drove the dragon, and that would go a long way to getting his body back.

"You no like me?"

The question startled Noah. There was a note of hurt in those words that upset Noah. He knew Byrd shared his thoughts, but he hadn't realized how closely the dragon could hear them. "*It's not that I don't like you.*" Noah searched for a way to explain so Byrd would understand. Remembering the way Byrd had shared his instincts and knowledge, Noah opened himself and dumped all of his feelings on Byrd—his frustration at being locked away from the world and his fear of the changes in his life.

The little dragon stopped on the steps and shivered in response. "*I sorry.*" Shame and regret filled his words.

Noah let out a sigh as he pushed his emotions away. "*Don't be sorry,*" he soothed the dragon and urged him back into motion. "*We're both going through some shocking changes right now, but we'll get through them together.*"

Byrd stopped again. "*Together?*"

"Yes Byrd, together." A wave of joy washed over Noah as Byrd's mood lightened. "*Now, let's go help Kara with the bed.*"

"Kara nice," Byrd chirped as he started up the steps after the woman. "*We likes her.*"

Noah would have smiled if he could have. "*Yes Byrd, she is, and we most certainly do.*"

Following Kara into the room, Byrd stopped in the doorway as Kara went over to the mattress and pulled it away from the wall. It teetered precariously on its edge, and Byrd was suddenly filled with a fear of Kara being hurt by the falling bedding.

"No, Byrd!" Noah cried, trying to stop the small dragon. He could see the disaster they were heading into, but the instinct to protect Kara was stronger than rational thought.

Rushing to her side to stabilize the bedding, his wing hit her in the leg, knocking her knee loose.

She squealed as she lost her balance and tumbled to the floor.

The little dragon squeaked in surprised and shoved his shoulders into the twin-sized mattress, trying to protect her, but it was too heavy. The large pad landed on them, squishing them both to the floor.

Byrd gasped for breath as he shifted under the bedding, trying to turn to check on the fallen woman. "Kara!" he chirped, looking for her.

Kara's hands came up and caught the small dragon by the tail before his frantic search got out of control. "Byrd!" she gasped as she held on to him.

He froze as the feel of her fingers on his scales sent shivers up his body.

Noah's mind reeled from the amount of endorphins Byrd's frantic dash had released. It was unlike anything he had ever experienced as a human. He panted, trying to get a grip on things, but Byrd's emotions ran rampant over him. The need to make sure Kara was okay was almost painful.

Releasing his tail, Kara pushed the mattress off them. "I'm okay, Byrd," she said as she raised herself up onto her elbows.

Byrd twisted around and plowed his head into her chest, inspecting her.

Kara laughed as she fell backwards. She caught his head and pushed it away. "I'm fine," she said as she ran her hand down his neck. A concerned look crossed her face as she pulled her hand back. She rubbed her fingers together as she looked at them.

Turning to see what she had found, Byrd sniffed at the smudges on her fingers. *Dirt.* Seeing nothing wrong with it, he turned his attention back to Kara and sniffed her, looking for injuries.

"I'm fine," Kara said pushing him back farther, "but you need a bath."

Byrd gave her a disgruntled look as she pushed the mattress back and got up from the floor.

Feeling the dragon's disgust at the idea of a bath, Noah shook himself free of the chemicals in his system and intervened before Byrd could make his feelings known. "*Wait, Byrd.*"

Byrd froze at the interruption of his thoughts. "*No bath.*"

"*Why not?*" Noah worked to lock his legs before the dragon could bolt from the room.

"*No bath!*" Byrd fought against Noah for control. The fight made them dance around.

The movement caught Kara's attention. "Are you all right?"

Byrd danced away from her as he fought with Noah for control. "No bath!" he chirped.

Kara stopped and stared at him.

Flashes of Raven taking baths bombarded Noah. She'd enjoyed taking long, luxurious baths with candles and bubbles. They'd relaxed her mind, but they'd bored Byrd to tears. "*No, Byrd!*" Noah cried, understanding the dragon's resistance. He thought a bath meant a long soak in water. "*Wash!*"

"*Wash?*" Byrd asked as he stopped struggling.

"*Yes,*" Noah answered. "*A bath, as in washing.*" Recalling a time he'd been forced into a bath by a broken showerhead, he showed Byrd a different type of bath than he knew.

"Wash?" Byrd asked out loud.

"Yes," Kara said carefully. "To wash."

"Ask her for a shower," Noah prompted.

Byrd paused before voicing the request. "Shower?"

Kara gave him a confused look. "If you would rather have a shower, we could do that."

Relief flooded Byrd as he relaxed. He nodded his head.

"Then a shower it is," Kara said as she turned and led the way out of the room.

"Showers are good," Noah said, soothing the ruffled dragon as he followed Kara out of the bedroom.

KARA GLANCED BACK over her shoulder as Byrd followed her out of the bedroom. *Why doesn't he like baths?* She pondered this as she headed down the hall and into her bedroom. She had always enjoyed a nice, hot bath. Her dragon shivered, driving a smile to her face. Okay, *she* enjoyed a long, hot bath—her dragon tolerated it. Most dragons preferred moving water to still. It would make sense that Byrd wouldn't like a bath.

Opening the door, she let Byrd into her bathroom. Using the hall bath would have been preferable, but she hadn't had time to get it set up yet. Besides, her shower had a wand that would make washing Byrd a lot easier. "Come on, sweetheart." She held the door to the bathroom for him.

Byrd looked around the room before heading in. He took up most of the area between the tub and the counter.

Kara let out a sigh. When she'd chosen this place, she had been excited by how much space was in the master bathroom. Okay, so it wasn't one of those huge places with a Jacuzzi tub and a walk-in shower, but it had plenty of room with a mirror covering the entire wall and enough counter space for all of her things. Now that she had a dragon in that area, it seemed tiny. Letting go of that slightly depressing thought, she wiggled past Byrd to the tub. Pulling the shower wand lose from the wall, she dropped it into the tub and sat on the edge to adjust the water. "So, how hot do you like your showers?"

Byrd shifted around in the small space to face her. "Hot?"

Kara just smiled. "How about we start at warm, and you can tell me if it's too cold?" When Byrd nodded, Kara played with the knobs until it was cooler than she would have picked, but still warm. "Okay."

Byrd sniffed at the spray. Reaching a foot into the tub, he batted at the water.

Smiling, Kara reached over and patted him on the shoulder. "Why don't you go on and get in there? I'll get some soap."

Batting at the spray again, Byrd hopped into the tub. With the water now hitting him in the chest, he snapped at it, trying to bite the stream.

Giggling, Kara reached up and pulled her loofah and bodywash down. "Now, be still." Grabbing the sprayer, she pointed the water at the little dragon.

After one more attempt to catch the water, Byrd dropped his head and let Kara soak him down.

Once he was damp, Kara dropped the wand back into the tub and squirted an ample amount of soap on the loofah. A moment of squeezing gave her a rich lather.

Byrd arched his neck in pleasure as she slid the loofah over him, working the soap across his scales.

Sliding her fingers up his neck, Kara stopped when she hit something hard. The bite of magic tingled against her skin. Surprised by the unusual item, she slid her finger along the leather band wrapped around Byrd's neck. "I completely forgot about this." Dropping her loofah, she grabbed the collar and tried to turn it so she could reach the buckle hidden under Byrd's boney crest. "Let me get this off you so we don't ruin it."

"*No!*" Byrd screeched, startling Kara into releasing the band. Jumping out of her hands, he crammed himself into the far corner of the tub as she jerked back. "*Mine!*"

Surprised, Kara raised her hands up between them, unsure how to respond to the dragon's adamant reaction. "Okay," she said meekly. "You can keep it on."

Slowly, Byrd relaxed back down into the tub.

Kara picked up the loofah and reached for him again.

Byrd flinched away.

"It's okay, Byrd. I'm not going to touch it," she reassured him while she rubbed the soap down his side. As she worked, she stole glances at the leather band around his neck. The black leather blended into his hide so well that it was hard to see if you weren't looking for it. Curiosity ate at her. *Why is he wearing a collar? Why doesn't he want it off?* She recalled the tingle of magic she'd felt as her hand brushed it. *What does it do?* More questions swirled in her head as she washed him, but his reaction to her touching it kept her from asking.

A musical note broke into Kara's musing. It took her a moment to realize her new doorbell had just been rung. "The pizza!" she yelled as she remembered the food they were waiting for. Jumping up from the tub, she raced out of the room. How could she have forgotten about food? "I'm coming!" she yelled as the doorbell rang again. Grabbing the door, she yanked it open before the guy could leave. "Sorry!" she huffed as she leaned on the door.

"It's cool," the pizza guy said as he pulled open his bag to get her food. "That's $34.85."

Shaking her head, she cleared the fluff from her brain. "Hang on while I get my purse." Backing away from the door, Kara tripped over something large. She shrieked as she fell over the unknown object. It took her a moment to realize the large, wet thing was Byrd.

He sniffed at her for a moment before turning his attention to the guy at the door.

Cursing to herself, Kara pushed up from the floor and went to get cash from her purse. She hadn't considered the possibility of Byrd following her out of the bathroom. Glancing back at him, she rolled her eyes. Not only was he dripping with suds, he'd backed the pizza guy out onto the porch. "Byrd!" she called as she went to save the poor man.

Byrd glanced at her but turned his head back to the man standing on the very edge of the porch.

Reaching out, she grabbed him by the collar around his neck and pulled him back before the delivery guy bolted. "Enough," she said, pushing him behind her.

Byrd circled around her and looked up at the guy from her other side.

She smiled warmly at the man. "Sorry about that." She held out the money for him to take. "He's just excited about the food."

The man chuckled as he took the cash and pulled the pizzas out. "I completely understand. Do you need change?"

Kara shook her head as she took the food. "No, keep it."

"Thanks, ma'am," he tipped his cap. "I hope you and your boyfriend enjoy it." Before Kara could correct the man's assumption, he was gone.

Kara let out a deep sigh and looked back at the small dragon. He was still soaking wet, but at least he was dripping soap on her porch and not on her living room carpet. Squatting down, she rested the stack of pizzas on her knee and reached out to scratch Byrd's head. "What am I going to do with you?"

Byrd ignored her touch and shoved his nose into the boxes, sniffing.

Letting out a laugh, Kara grabbed the boxes and stood up. "Come on," she said leading the way into the house. "Let's finish getting you cleaned up so we can eat."

"BYRD!" Noah yelled, frustrated that the dragon hadn't listened to him since Kara had bolted from the bathroom.

Overjoyed with the prospect of food, Byrd continued to ignore Noah as he started into the house behind Kara.

Noah's irritation got the better of him. "*Stop!*" Concentrating hard, he locked his knees, forcing the dragon to stop.

"What?" Byrd snapped back.

"Get back outside!" Noah yelled.

Byrd stood in the doorway. "*Why?*" His eyes followed Kara as she made her way through the house.

"Because you're soaking wet!" Noah growled. "*We're going to ruin Kara's carpet.*" He eased his control over the little dragon.

Shifting from foot to foot, Byrd stood on the threshold, unsure what to do. Desire pushed at him. "*Hungry!*" he whined, watching as Kara set down the boxes filled with yummy-smelling stuff on the bar.

"I know you're hungry—so am I," Noah snapped, "*but we need to stop and wait. Ask Kara to get something to dry us off with.*"

"Hungry!" Byrd snapped angrily. He danced around in the doorway but didn't go in.

Noah sighed heavily in exasperation. There was no way he was going to make the single-minded dragon understand the complex social concept of being polite. Well, at least not until he'd gotten some food in him. But at least Byrd was listening to him enough to stay where he was and not drip soap all over the carpet.

Kara grabbed up a dishtowel from a box. "I'm sorry," she said as she rushed back to the door where Byrd was waiting impatiently.

Backing up, Byrd wiggled as Kara got closer. "Hungry," he whined again.

"Just give her a moment, Byrd," Noah soothed him. *"She'll get us dry, and then we can go in."*

Unwilling to wait anymore, Byrd shook violently.

Raising the towel up to protect herself, Kara squeaked as soap and water flew off the small dragon, covering everything around him. Sighing, she dropped her hands and shot Byrd a sharp look. "Really?" she asked in disbelief.

"Hungry," Byrd answered, prancing in place. He gave her a desperate, pleading look before glancing inside to where she'd left the boxes.

Letting out an exasperated sigh that matched Noah's, Kara shook her head. "Go on." She waved Byrd inside. Taking the towel, she brushed the soap and water from the front of her shirt.

Byrd stood his ground for a moment longer.

Noah felt the pleading thoughts swirling around Byrd's mind. *"Go on,"* Noah said, echoing Kara's words.

Squeaking in joy, Byrd raced inside, eyes trained on the boxes.

"No, Byrd," Noah yelled as he felt the muscles in his legs bunch as the dragon prepared to spring on to the counter.

Stopping mid-leap, Byrd growled. *"Hungry!"*

Racing up behind him, Kara grabbed the top box on

the stack. "Here!" Flipping the pizza open, she slung it down on the kitchen floor.

Byrd attacked the food with a vigor that made Kara jump back and check to make sure she still had all her fingers.

"Calm down!" Noah snapped at the overexcited dragon. *"It's not going anywhere."*

Byrd paused and growled at Noah before shoving his face back into the food, gulping it down without tasting it.

"You're going to make us sick!" Noah snapped again.

After another growl, Byrd slowed his pace just slightly.

Letting out a mental sigh, Noah mentally shook his head and let the dragon go. *"We're going to talk about your manners later,"* he promised.

KARA STOOD there in shock and watched the small dragon devouring pizza. For a moment, she had been hopeful that Byrd and Noah were starting to communicate, but this reaction made her think otherwise. No matter their form, most dragons retained their humanity through their shifts, but Byrd's reaction was what she would have expected from a wild animal, not a highly intelligent being. The fact that he hadn't leaped up on the counter and helped himself had astounded her.

Seeing that he was almost done with the first pizza, Kara opened the second one and dropped it onto the floor next to him.

He grunted in acknowledgement but didn't stop eating.

Taking one of the slices from the final pizza box, she folded it in half and took a bite. She watched Byrd finish the first pizza and start on the second. *For such a little thing, he can really put food away!* A stray thought hit her. It made sense that he was ravenous. The past day had been really long for Byrd. And with as much pizza as he was eating, he was in for one hell of a food coma tonight. Kara finished her slice as she watched Byrd gorge himself. Tucking the top down on the last pizza, she took it with her as she headed towards the steps. It was rude to hoard her food, but she had things she needed to do upstairs. If she left the rest down here, Byrd would have it devoured before she could get back to it.

Heading into her room, she dropped the pizza on her bed and went in to shut the water off. She let out an amused laugh as she looked over the mess Byrd had made. There was soap and water everywhere. She added 'mopping' to her list of chores to do before bed. But first, she needed to get her guest room put together. Then, she could start on the rest of the house. So far, this little dragon was more of a pain in the ass than she had expected.

Chapter 5

The morning light crept across Kara's bed, waking her. She rolled over, trying to hang on to the evaporating wisps of her dreams, but the morning sun burned them from her memory. The only thing that stuck was a vague feeling of scales against her skin. Cracking an eye, she glared at the bare panes of glass letting the light shine into her room. That was something she was going to have to fix today. Waking up to an east-facing window blazing sun across her bed wasn't her idea of an excellent start to the day. She added 'hanging curtains' to her seemingly endless to-do list, but it was a lot further down the list than she would have liked. There were more pressing issues to tend to first.

Grumbling, Kara pulled herself out of bed and dug in the box next to her bed for her bathrobe. She pulled it on over her pajamas as she headed for the kitchen, hoping Byrd wasn't awake yet. She needed her daily dose of caffeine before she could face the little dragon and his issues. Her mind turned over the events of yesterday and her plans for today as she walked.

She'd thought long and hard about the poor dragon after she'd put him to bed. He hadn't been much help in anything after his huge meal. It had been all she could do to get the pizza sauce cleaned off him before coaxing him into the freshly made bed to pass out. He seemed more at ease with himself than when she had first met him, but there was still a long way to go. The most important part was to get him to relax and trust her so they could work on getting him in touch with his human side. She had come up with the perfect idea last night before she had fallen asleep—a nice flight was just what he needed, but she had to clear her schedule first.

Thoughts of her day escaped her as she came up on Byrd's open door. "Byrd?" she called as she poked her head into the room. Her eyes fell on the rumpled bed. Stepping into the room, she glanced around for her guest. *Not here?* His bed was used, or at least messed up, but he wasn't anywhere to be seen. Gathering his pillows from the floor, she fluffed them up and placed them back on the bed where they belonged. As she straightened out the bedding, she paused. Something wasn't right. The quilt was missing. She looked around for the wayward bedding, but it wasn't anywhere to be found. Dropping the sheets, she went to find her houseguest.

She pondered over his whereabouts as she made her way downstairs. He had probably gotten hungry and come down to help himself to some leftover pizza. A smile crept across her face as she recalled his foraging trip that had left her kitchen in a mess yesterday. Hopefully, he hadn't gotten his head stuck in anything this morning. "Byrd?" she called as her feet hit the carpet. She glanced towards the kitchen, but it was empty.

Turning to her living room, she smiled when she finally found her missing dragon. He was curled up in the corner of the living room. The blanket from his bed was wrapped around him as if he'd been nesting. Kara felt her dragon stretch. It had been a long time since she had allowed herself to nest in anything, and the desire to go over and cuddle up next to Byrd pulled at her.

She started over but stopped when something caught her eye. The cushions on the couch were missing. Shocked, she turned back to look at Byrd and his nest. The blanket covered most of it, but she could just see the edge of a cushion poking out of his nest. Horror filled her as her mind, doing quick mental calculations, determined that Byrd's nest was wider and flatter than the couch cushions should have been. "Byrd!" Kara gasped as she rushed over and flipped the edge of his nest up.

Byrd raised his head and looked at her sleepily.

What Kara found under his blanket made her want to cry. Yes, the cushions of her couch were making up the padding for his nest, but they weren't whole anymore. "*How could you?*" Kara cried as she dropped to her knees next to the pile of torn-up foam and cotton batting. "My couch!"

Byrd just blinked.

Biting back her anger, Kara got up and turned away. The desire to scream welled inside her, but she schooled herself into not crying or yelling as she forced herself to walk away. She needed to stay calm despite what damage he had done. Yelling at Byrd would only upset him, and she needed him to trust her so she could help him. Flying into a rage was not going to do either of them any good. Summoning the patience of a saint, she turned and pinned the little dragon with an angry stare. "I'm not happy, Byrd," she said as calmly as she could through clenched teeth. "We will talk about this later."

Turning away from him, she left the little dragon to his

own devices. She couldn't deal with this right now. Maybe after she had a hot shower, she would have her temper well enough under control to explain things to him. Then again, maybe not. She had loved that couch.

MOVEMENT and a loud cry woke Noah from his dreams. Turning his head, he found Kara standing over him. Her face was red as a beet, and she looked on the verge of tears.

"*How could you?*" she cried as she dropped to her knees next to him. Her hands touched the edge of his bed but pulled back with clenched fists. "My couch!"

Noah blinked at her again, not understanding what was going on. *What in the world was she talking about?* Blinking again, he looked down at the bed he was lying on. It was really comfortable, but it wasn't the bed he remembered going to sleep on. Movement from Kara had him turning back to her. Her spine was ramrod straight as she turned away. The quiver in her shoulders gave away exactly how mad she was, but Noah didn't understand why she was pissed.

She took a few steps away before turning and glaring at him.

Noah cringed at the anger in her eyes.

"I'm not happy, Byrd," she said through clenched teeth. "We will talk about this later." With a sharp step, she was off and up the stairs before he could say anything.

Unsure what was going on, Noah looked around. This was not the room where he'd gone to bed last night. This was most definitely Kara's living room, but he didn't remember coming down. Getting up, he stumbled out of the nest and looked around for what had caused Kara's outburst. She had mentioned the couch, so he turned to look at it. The cushions were missing. A sinking feeling hit Noah, and he turned to look at the nest he'd just crawled from.

Flipping the covers back, he revealed a mess of shredded batting and foam pieces. *"Byrd!"* Noah roared. He startled himself when the sound actually echoed in the room. It had been the first time he had been in control since Byrd had taken over his body. He felt the sleepy mind of the dragon stretch as it woke up. "Wake up *now*, Byrd!" Noah shook his head, rousting the dragon. "Explain this!" Noah's senses dimmed a little as the dragon woke up and reclaimed their body. Noah tried to hang on, but Byrd had more control in this form.

Byrd rumbled his disgust in being awake.

"Don't give me that," Noah snapped. "*Explain this mess!"*

Looking over the nest he had made, Byrd shrugged. "*Comfy."*

Noah bristled at the answer. "*What do you mean* comfy*? We tore up her couch!"*

Letting out a jaw-cracking yawn, Byrd shrugged and headed back into the nest. He curled up and draped the end of his tail across his nose.

"Oh no!" Noah snapped at the dragon. "*We are not going back to sleep."*

Byrd grumbled and cracked open an eye to glare out at the world.

Noah could feel the dragon's annoyance, but he wasn't going to let him get away with this. Misbehaving was one thing, but destruction was something else. "*We are going to get up and clean this mess up."*

"Why?" Byrd grumbled and rolled over in the bedding. "*Comfy."*

"I don't care if it's comfy," Noah ranted. "*We can't just lie here! Kara is pissed off that we tore up her couch."*

A confused feeling came from the dragon. *"Kara's upset?"* Byrd rolled to his stomach and looked over to where Kara had disappeared upstairs. Curiosity rolled through him, and he stood up to go see why she was unhappy.

"No, Byrd." Noah reached for the dragon, trying to stop him. They both were surprised when they stopped after a few steps.

"Why not?"

"Kara's upset that we tore up her couch. If we go up now, it would make her more upset," Noah explained.

Byrd sat down on his haunches. "*Why?*"

Letting out a sigh, Noah tried to think of a way to explain it. "*Do you remember a time someone destroyed something of yours?*"

Turning his thoughts inwards, Byrd thought about it.

Noah tracked the dragon's thoughts as he searched through Raven's memories. "*There!*" Noah stopped him at the memory of someone breaking something important to Raven. "*Do you remember how that made Raven feel?*" Anger filled Noah as Byrd relived the experience. He breathed through the feeling, soothing Byrd as he went.

"Mad," Byrd finally answered.

"And we just tore up something that was important to Kara," Noah pointed out gently. "*How do you think that made her feel?*"

Byrd's wings dropped as he envisioned Kara feeling the way Raven had. He whimpered in regret.

"It's all right, Byrd," Noah calmed the dragon. "*Kara's going to be mad at us for a while, but there is something we can do to help."*

"Fix couch?" Byrd said hopefully, perking up.

Noah chuckled to himself. "*No, we can't fix the couch."*

Byrd's wings drooped again.

"But if we clean up the mess, Kara might forgive us for tearing up the cushions."

Byrd nodded his agreement.

"Come on," Noah coaxed the dragon. *"Let's see if we can find some trash bags from the kitchen and pick this up before she comes back down."*

DUSTING on the last of her makeup, Kara stood back from the bathroom mirror and considered herself. The silvery tank top and smoky shadow she'd picked brought out the subtle gray tones in her eyes, making them darker than her normal hazel. They suited her dark mood. Her original plan for the day was to start by pulling out some of her pans and making breakfast, but coming down to find that Byrd had destroyed her couch had changed that. The hot steam from the shower had helped ease her anger, but she'd taken much longer than she'd originally intended. Now it was going to have to be fast food before going into the office for a while.

Heading out to her bedroom, she grabbed her cardigan and pulled the thin, black material into place. Normally she would have coupled this set with a wispy, black skirt and heels, but today she chose to go with some dark slacks and low pumps. Despite the fact she was still upset with Byrd, Kara had decided to follow through with her plans to take Byrd flying. For that, she would need something a little less formal. These clothes would be easier for her to change out of when they got to the park.

Kara shivered as her dragon stretched in anticipation. She smiled as she checked herself one last time in the mirror. The whole purpose in going out today was to get

Byrd to relax, but she was looking forward to the outing, too. It'd been a long time since she had been out in scales, and after these last two days, she could really use the time to unwind. There was nothing like wind across your scales to ease your troubles away. Taking a deep breath, Kara prepared herself for the mess in the living room. *I will not be mad. I will not be mad. I will not be mad.*

The sound of ripping plastic broke into Kara's calming chant. Anger filled her as she rushed downstairs to see what that blasted dragon was destroying this time. She prayed it wasn't something irreplaceable. As she turned the corner into the living room, she stopped. Her brain froze as she tried to make sense of the scene in front of her. The living room was a disaster. The nest Byrd made had exploded, spewing bits of foam and fluff everywhere. And Byrd was in the middle of it all with a mouthful of foam, trying desperately to get the top of a garbage bag open.

Gasping in surprise, Kara raised her hand to her mouth as emotions rolled over her. She was both pissed that he'd made more of a mess and elated that he had thought enough to attempt cleaning up what he'd done. Her dragon stirred, adding another emotion to the mix, but she pushed it away as fast as she could and refocused on the fact that he was her patient. She was supposed to be helping him get his act together, not starting to care for him… no matter how cute he looked with bits of stuffing stuck to the ridges on his back.

The small noise she'd made drew Byrd's attention away from the bag. He looked up and found her standing there. Dropping the mouthful of padding, he squeaked loudly and rushed over to her.

Kara dropped down to catch the small dragon before he plowed into her legs and bowled her over.

"I sorry," he whined as he rubbed his face into Kara.

Wrapping her hands around the distressed dragon, she caught him before she fell. That emotion she had pushed away plowed back into her. Biting it back, she set a firm look on her face. She held him for a moment before grabbing the edges of his frill and pulling him back. His dark eyes shone with remorse, softening the anger inside her and strengthening that other emotion she didn't want to face. After a minute of searching his face, she spoke. "I'm still irritated with you."

Byrd whined and tried to lower his head, but she held him in place.

"But the fact that you tried to clean up helps."

Hope glimmered in his eyes.

"Do you promise not to do this again?"

Byrd emphatically nodded his head. "We be good!"

A smile softened the stern look on Kara's face. "Then I'll forgive you."

Squeaking with joy, Byrd plowed into her, knocking her over as he nuzzled her.

The sincere emotions rolling off the dragons were overwhelming and infectious. Kara laughed as she landed on her back. After a moment of catching her breath, she reached up and patted him on the shoulder. "Enough." She pushed him back so she could get up.

Byrd backed up but didn't go far.

"Come on," she said as she got up from the floor. "We have stuff to do today."

Prancing in place, Byrd looked back at the mess he'd made.

"We'll clean that up later," she reassured him. "Right now, we have to go." She slipped the strap of her purse over her shoulder and opened the door.

Byrd waffled for a moment longer before heading out the door.

Kara watched him go to the car before turning and locking up. She wasn't sure what to make of him. Responsibility was not an instinctual thing. The fact that he had shown it proved that he was somehow in touch with Noah, but she hadn't seen any personality of the human half coming through. Well, not unless Noah acted like a three-year-old child. And she couldn't see anyone making it very far in Eternity with that type of attitude. It was a start, but they still had a long way to go.

THE JOY and excitement flowing from Byrd was hard for Noah to get past. It washed out his thoughts, leaving him in a strange state of euphoria. He had never experienced the world quite the way Byrd saw it. The pure, undiluted emotions of the dragon overwhelmed Noah. And to make it even harder to handle, Byrd's emotions could jump from one extreme to the other in a heartbeat.

When Noah had laid into him for destroying Kara's couch, an overwhelming anxiety had filled Byrd. It was enough to make Noah want to bawl his eyes out. He had managed to get Byrd together enough to try to clean up the mess, but the negative emotions were almost crippling.

When Kara had come down and forgiven them, Byrd's emotions jumped the other way—so much so that, had Noah been in control, he wouldn't have been able to breathe. Now that Byrd was happy again, whatever was driving his emotions was settling down.

Noah drew a cleansing breath and considered Byrd as the little dragon got into the car and waited for Kara to take them wherever she wanted to go. Noah was astounded by the range of emotion Byrd felt. The fact that his emotions had jumped from highs to lows and back again in no time at all reminded Noah of a woman with a bad case of PMS. Any little thing could drive her to either end of the emotional spectrum. That's exactly the way Noah felt at that moment.

He followed Byrd's mind as the dragon looked out the window, watching the world rush by. There weren't any real thoughts, just feelings and impressions. It gave him a lot more insight into the inner workings of dragons. If he ever wanted to regain some control over his life, he was going to have to find a way to control Byrd, and the best way to do that was through his emotions. But Noah couldn't just lead the dragon around. He was going to have to find a way to coexist with him.

"Are you hungry?"

Kara's words broke into both Noah's and Byrd's thoughts.

Byrd jumped up and turned circles on the seat. "*Yes!*" he chirped excitedly.

Kara giggled and laid her hand on Byrd's shoulder, pushing him back down. "Settle down before you make us wreck."

Byrd gave under her gentle touch and sank to the seat.

A wave of emotion hit Noah, leaving him reeling. Trying to put a name to the emotion was hard. Respect, loyalty, and devotion were as close as he could come. A second epiphany struck Noah. Byrd would do anything for Kara.

"We likes her."

Byrd's thought echoed through Noah as the dragon stretched his neck across the gap between the seats and settled his chin on Kara's lap.

Her hand came down and patted him before going back to the steering wheel.

Noah chuckled softly. He agreed with the dragon, but

he was reluctant to say so. Intellectually, Noah knew Kara was only there because Daniel had ordered her to help them. This was her job. When it was over, she would leave them for her next patient. But the instincts pushing at him insisted she cared and wouldn't leave him. The opposing concepts left him conflicted about where he stood in the situation. It was hard to deal with the irrational attachment he was starting to feel for the woman. Warmth washed over him from Byrd, calming the distressing thoughts.

Noah smiled. "*Yes, we do.*" Making that announcement to Byrd didn't change the conflict he felt, but it gave strength to the side he wasn't sure was good for his heart.

"So, what do you want?" Kara asked.

Noah looked up. Through the window, he could see the menu board of the drive thru.

"Food!" Byrd chirped and wiggled around, trying to get into her lap and out the window.

Kara grabbed his collar and held him back from jumping out the window.

"Settle down, Byrd," Noah scolded as he tried to make them look at the menu. It was impossible to focus on the words while Byrd danced around in excitement.

"Sit!" Noah snapped out loud, startling them all.

Byrd froze in Kara's arms.

Kara's eyes widened in surprise.

"Sorry," Noah chirped. He glanced over the menu. "One of those egg sandwich things, some hash browns, and…" he paused, debating. He really wanted a cup of coffee, but he wasn't sure how it would affect Byrd's already-hyper mentality. "Some juice," he finished before crawling out of Kara's lap and curling onto the seat.

A hint of fear brushed against his mind. He drew in a deep breath and soothed the scared dragon. "*I'm sorry.*"

The fear in Byrd uncurled a little, but he was still wary of Noah.

Noah sighed again. "*I know you're happy and excited about getting food, but we can't jump around like that in the car.*"

Byrd cocked his head in question.

"*We can cause Kara to wreck, or hurt her.*"

"*No hurt Kara!*" Byrd growled at him.

"*I know you wouldn't intentionally hurt her, but you could do it accidently.*"

Byrd thought about it for a moment. "*Be calm in car.*"

"*Yes,*" Noah agreed. "*Be calm in the car.*"

Byrd nodded his head. He tilted it and paused in thought. "*You mad?*"

Noah chuckled. "*No, Byrd. I'm a little frustrated, but I'm not mad.*"

"*I sorry.*" Byrd wiggled in despair.

Noah drew in another calming breath. "*It's all right, Byrd. We'll get through this. Together.*"

"*Together!*" Byrd's thought echoed through Noah as if the little dragon had screamed it in this head.

The smell of impending breakfast drew Byrd's attention away from Noah. Uncurling from the seat, he wiggled in anticipation.

"*Byrd!*" Noah called, grabbing the dragon's attention.

Byrd froze. "*Yes?*"

"*Remember what we talked about?*"

The dragon thought about it for a second. "*Be calm in car?*"

"*Yes,*" Noah said, pleased that he remembered. "*It's time to be calm and wait.*"

Byrd eyed the bags coming into the car and whined, sniffing at the savory smells filling the car. "*Hungry.*"

"*I know you're hungry, but we have to wait for Kara to give us the food,*" Noah explained. "*Not all of that is ours.*"

Byrd watched the bags as Kara set them down on the floorboard in front of him. She said something to him in a warning tone, but he was too busy contemplating Noah's words to hear them. "*Not ours?*" he asked, confused.

"No," Noah continued. "*Part of that food is Kara's."*

At the mention of her name, Byrd looked up to the woman next to him. Her attention was focused on the traffic around them. "*Kara's?*"

"Yes, and if we eat it all, she won't get any."

A range of emotion rolled through Byrd.

Noah tried to track them, but it was hard to understand what the dragon was thinking. It knew what it wanted, but the fact that Noah had pointed out the needs of another set things in motion that Noah didn't understand.

"Come on, Byrd."

Kara's voice broke into whatever was running through the dragon's mind. He looked up at her.

"Let's go eat." Reaching down, she pulled the bags of food into her lap and balanced them as she got out of the car.

Byrd sat and stared at her.

"Go on," Noah urged.

Byrd followed her out of the car. He paused to look around. The small parking lot bordered a grassy area with a few picnic tables. He glanced up to find Kara already on her way to one of the tables with her load. A few loping strides had him up and on the bench of the table she'd chosen.

Noah was surprised as Byrd watched Kara separate out the food. The dragon wiggled in anticipation but made no move to take anything until Kara had everything unwrapped.

"There you go, sweetheart," Kara said as she tucked

the paper under the sandwich Noah had ordered. "All yours."

Byrd stared at her as she sat down and started eating.

The steam rising from the eggs made Noah's mouth water. He waited for the hungry dragon to attack the meal with the same gusto he'd had with the pizza last night, but Byrd held his ground, watching Kara eat her food. *"Byrd?"* Noah prompted. *"We can eat now."*

Byrd's eyes remained on Kara. *"Kara eat."*

"Kara is *eating,"* Noah pointed out.

"Kara's food," Byrd argued.

"No," Noah tried to reason with the dragon, *"Kara has her food. This is our food."*

Byrd looked over the meal laid out before him. *"Our food?"*

"Yes. Our food." Noah looked up at Kara. *"Kara has plenty of food. In fact, she's almost done. If we don't hurry, she'll be done before we are."*

Byrd looked over the dwindling meal on the other side of the table. Tentatively, he moved to take one of the hash browns Noah had ordered. When Kara didn't stop him, he chomped it down.

"See? She isn't going to keep you from your food. She has enough." Noah coaxed him into taking more of the meal.

Giving in to his grumbling belly, Byrd scarfed down the rest of his fare without complaint.

Noah mentally shook his head and relaxed, thinking about the dragon. Last night, there had been no stopping Byrd from taking what he wanted, but today it took coaxing to get him to eat. Something had changed in the dragon, but Noah wasn't sure what.

IT WAS a beautiful morning for a picnic. The sky was clear with just enough of a breeze to keep the bugs at bay. The shade of the tall pine trees made the table Kara had picked the perfect place to eat. She loved to come out here and watch the ducks in the distant pond float around, but today, she didn't notice them. Her mind was trained on the small dragon following her to the picnic table.

The heavy traffic had kept her from more than a quick glance at him while she drove, but she couldn't help but feel something significant had happened in the car. His sudden outburst had startled her. It also seemed to have startled him. And the order he'd given hadn't seemed like the same excited dragon she was getting used to. It had been serious and almost surly.

Was Noah a surly person? Kara didn't know much about Noah, only that he was a high-level mage with Eternity, and that he had been human before joining with Byrd. Images of an elderly man with white hair, siting in some dank vault and pouring over ancient tomes of magic, filled her mind.

She shook the thought away as preposterous. Eternity would never allow such valuable books to rot away in some damp dungeon. If anything, they were kept in a state-of-the-art facility with climate-controlled rooms and special lighting to keep them safe and whole. But the possibility of Noah being an aged man with white hair was more than slim. Noah wasn't a very common name in younger generations, and the most powerful mages had spent the better part of their lives perfecting their arts. Plus, the magic would have bleached the pigment from him. Why it bleached the color from humans but not dragons still puzzled scientists and mages alike.

Pushing that line of thought away, she peeled the paper around Byrd's sandwich back and laid it on the table.

"There you go, sweetheart. All yours." Looking back, she checked the bench before sitting down and starting in on her own food.

Picking up her sandwich, she bit into it. The sweetness of the croissant was the perfect contrast to the sharpness of the Swiss cheese and ham inside. It was one of her favorite breakfast foods. She closed her eyes and savored that first bite before getting down to the business of really eating. With the ravenous appetite Byrd had shown last night, she was going to have to hurry if she had any hope of keeping up with him.

Glancing at the dragon, she was surprised to find him watching her, his meal untouched. A note of concern tightened Kara's chest, but she forced herself to continue eating. The fact that Byrd hadn't dug into his food right away worried her. He had been so excited about it in the car. Her dragon supplied her with a single thought.

"Brooding."

Kara shook her head and nibbled at her food. "*He can't be brooding,*" she argued back. Brooding was bad. It would throw his system out of whack, making it harder for his two halves to connect. Plus, it meant that he saw her as a potential mate. She didn't want a mate!

"Are you sure?"

Looking back across the table, Kara studied him as she ate. A confused look sat on his face as he glanced between her and his food. She hated to admit it, but she did feel drawn to him. Then again, she had always had a bit of a soft spot for hard-luck cases, and his was the worst she had seen in a while. The fact that her dragon liked him made her job harder, but there was more to picking a mate than just listening to instincts. Byrd's childlike innocence was endearing—even when he was causing trouble—but it was the human half that concerned her. She knew nothing of

Noah. Who was he? What had his life been like before he'd joined with Byrd? What plans did he have for his future? All questions that needed answers.

Kara's heart fluttered when Byrd tipped his head over and carefully picked up one of his hash browns. She glanced over her meal. There wasn't much left, but the fact that the dragon hadn't waited until it was gone was a good sign. She peeked back up to find him scarfing down his food with the same enthusiasm he had given the pizza last night. Letting out a sigh of relief, she stuffed the last of her sandwich in her mouth. *He wasn't brooding; just talking with his other half.*

A soft crunching noise drew Kara's attention again.

Byrd had finished his food and was trying to get into the sealed cup of orange juice.

She drew a breath to stop him, but it was too late.

Juice squirted everywhere as he crunched through the thin plastic.

"Oh Byrd." She sighed as he licked the sticky liquid from the table. Shaking her head, she gathered up the trash and let the little dragon be. The spill had been an honest mistake, and there was no sense in reprimanding his uncouth behavior. Besides, if Noah were as surly as she suspected, he was probably already yelling at the poor dragon. She sighed and stood up to deal with the garbage.

Dumping the trash, she turned to call Byrd to the car, but he was no longer at the table. "Byrd?" she called, looking around for where he'd run off to. He was nowhere in sight. A zing of fear hit her as she scanned the park for him. Daniel was going to have her hide if she lost him. Taking an anxious step back towards the table, she called him again.

A scratching noise from the stand of pine trees drew her attention. Letting out a deep sigh, she relaxed when she caught sight of him. The feeling was short-lived, however, as she watched him lift his back leg against the tree. Spinning from the sight, she closed her eyes in utter humiliation. *Just when I thought he was making progress.*

Opening her eyes, she glanced around the mostly empty parking lot. There were a few people relaxing around the area, but no one was paying enough attention to catch Byrd watering the trees. *Thank goodness.* She sighed in relief. Now she just had to get him out of here before he broke any more public decency laws. Hopefully, this was a onetime thing and she could get Noah back in charge soon. Explaining society's standards for defecation was not a conversation she wanted to have with a being driven by instinct.

A touch on her leg drew her attention down to the little dragon. "Feel better?" she asked wryly.

Byrd looked up at her. "Yes," he chirped happily and went back to sniffing at the ground.

An exasperated smile curled the corner of her mouth as she shook her head. The dragon had completely missed the sarcasm in her question. Chuckling softly to herself, she let the matter go and headed to her car. It was clear that his instincts were back in control. "Come on," she called to him as she opened the door.

Byrd hopped into the passenger's seat and circled until he was comfortable enough to lie down.

Shutting the door, Kara let out another laugh at the absurdity her life was turning into. Never in her years of therapy had she run into someone as impulsive as Byrd. Curbing that impulsivity was going to be the hard part.

She couldn't just yell at Byrd for his crazy urges. Most of them were natural things that he needed to be comfortable. Plus, scolding him could upset him, and that would throw his system further out of balance. She had to find a way to correct him gently. But that could get tricky. She needed to find out more about his human half. Hopefully, she'd be able to pull Noah's latest psychological evaluations and personnel records when she got to her office. That would help her figure out how to deal with any additional embarrassing situations.

As she circled the car, she prayed nothing else would happen before she figured him out, but the chances of that were slim. It was still early, and they had a lot to do today.

Chapter 6

The morning sun glittered off the front of the glass-and-steel structure. Byrd sat on the car seat and stared at it in awe.

"We're here," Kara said as she pulled into a parking space near the front of the building.

"Where?" Noah asked, staring at the impressive building. He'd never seen anything like it. It had to be at least ten stories tall and looked like someone had taken a gigantic, latticework egg and dropped it in the middle of a park at an odd cant. One side was flat, and there was a huge hole built into the top where the point of the egg should have been. It was an impressive piece of modern architecture that boggled the mind.

Kara giggled at the awe in his voice. "Work," she said as she got out and held the door open. "I have to pick up a few things."

Shaken by her laughter, Byrd pulled his eyes away from the amazing structure and climbed out of the car.

Noah glanced around as they followed Kara across the parking lot and onto the sidewalk leading to the building. A few months ago, he'd heard the medical division had finally moved into their new location, but he hadn't had a reason to check it out. The medic on staff at Eternity's main office had been able to cover most of his needs. He had, however, been impressed to hear that the new building was state-of-the-art—complete with high-tech solar heating and wind turbines—but he'd never expected it to look so avant-garde.

"Pretty!" Byrd chirped.

Noah chuckled. *"It's very pretty indeed."*

Following Kara into the building, they paused for a moment to look around the lobby. It was just as impressive as the outside of the building. Noah's eyes were pulled to the left where a rock waterfall dominated the wall. The water tumbled into a shallow pool that flowed out through a sunken channel, mimicking a small river as it cut across the center of the room. An array of lush plants softened the hard lines of the manmade feature, and a wide bridge arched gracefully over the center. Along the edges of the water were benches where people could relax and enjoy the beauty of the room. A second-story walkway circled the open space, and Noah was sure the view from up there was spectacular. The babbling water echoing through the room made the extraordinary area surprisingly calming despite the people bustling about. *Very impressive.*

Pulling his attention away from the room, he hurried to catch up with Kara.

Once across the short bridge, she turned to the right, towards an alcove that held two elevators. There was a surprisingly large group waiting.

Glancing at the crowd, Kara looked down and gave Byrd a pained smile. "I didn't realize there would be so many people," she explained. "I usually get here a lot earlier." She looked back at the line for the elevator. "Would you rather take the stairs?"

Noah counted the people he could see. There were a lot. "How high?" he asked. He was surprised that the words had actually come out as sound.

"Six floors," Kara answered.

Noah considered the options. It would probably be faster to walk than it would be to wait for a ride up. He poked at Byrd, but the dragon was too awed by the number of people and the new space to have an opinion. Nodding his head, Noah made the call for them. "Let's walk."

He turned away from the crowd and wandered back into the open space of the lobby. It was surprising to have control of his body again. He stretched his wings before folding them in against his back once more. It was a weird sensation, but something he was getting used to. The desire to go sniff at some of the plants overwhelmed him, and he gave in before Byrd stepped up and took over. The depth of the smells he could now pick up was amazing.

"Byrd," Kara called from behind him.

Byrd whipped his head around to look at her.

"This way." She nodded to the far wall.

Noah let out a sigh as Byrd took over and loped over to meet her. It had been nice having control while it lasted. A questioning feeling from the dragon hit him, and he laughed. "*Yes, Byrd, I do like being in control.*"

"*Why?*" Byrd asked as he caught up to Kara leading the way up the steps.

"*Well…*" Noah paused as he tried to find a way to explain it to the dragon. It was hard to describe what it was like, riding around as a passenger in his own body. It wasn't like he was helpless or frightened anymore. Those feelings had passed after he started understanding Byrd's mind.

This was more like a part of him was missing. "*It makes me feel whole,*" he finished. That probably wasn't the best way to answer Byrd's question, but Noah felt the dragon consider his words. After a few moments, he felt Byrd let go.

Noah stumbled as he tripped up the steps. He paused to catch his balance before he landed on his face and slid down the stairs. The fact that Byrd had relinquished control had surprised him.

"You okay?"

Noah looked up to find Kara had stopped a few steps ahead of him. She watched him with concern in her eyes.

"I'm fine," Noah reassured her and started up the steps again. It took him a few tries to get all of his legs working together to climb the steps. It was different than walking on flat ground, but he quickly got the hang of it and was soon hopping up the steps with ease. When he reached the top of the steps, he turned back to Kara. She stood on the stairs, watching him with a look of confusion on her face.

"Are you coming?" Noah called down. He turned circles on the landing, getting used to the way his muscles worked. Watching as Byrd moved them around was a lot different than actually doing it himself. He stretched his wings again, feeling the pull of new muscles. That adventurous part of him wanted to jump up to the railing and see what it was like to fly.

"Flying fun!"

Noah chuckled. "*I bet it is.*" He tucked his wings back in. "*But not now.*"

He could feel Byrd's disappointment.

"Kara has stuff to do right now," he explained. "*We can ask her if we can go flying later.*"

Byrd let out a rumble of agreement before settling back down at the edge of Noah's perception.

It was the most distance he'd had from the dragon since he'd woken up to find Byrd still sleeping. After having the dragon pressed so close to his mind, it felt a little odd to be alone in his own skull. Shaking the thought from his head, Noah looked back down to where Kara had stalled out on the steps. Her mouth hung slightly open as if she were ready to say something.

"You coming?" Noah asked again, turning another circle. It felt good to move about under his own volition again.

"Yes," Kara squeaked and hurried up the steps.

Noah paused and looked down at her. Her voice had cracked with a note of surprise. He looked around for what had startled her but couldn't see anything unusual. He turned another circle as he waited. The joy of being able to move again made him giddy. As Kara topped the steps, he slipped around her and brushed up against her legs in passing. If he had been human, he would have grabbed her and jumped her feet into motion to some snappy Latin beat. *I bet she can dance a mean samba!* Byrd's wholehearted agreement set Noah's toes tapping, and he wiggled after her towards a stairwell door.

With Kara holding the door, Noah slipped passed her and danced up to the sixth floor, humming an off-key tune as he went. When he got to her floor, he sat down to wait for the woman, claws tapping out the catchy rhythm against the tile floor.

Slowly, Kara followed him up the steps, a perplexed look on her face.

"Come on," Noah called to her as she climbed the last set of steps. "Sixth floor, right?"

Not waiting for an answer, he stood up and pushed the door open with his shoulder. It opened onto a carpeted lobby. Two plush couches were arranged against one wall, and a high counter was tucked neatly into the far corner. One whole side of the room was made up of the glass-and-metal work seen from the outside of the building.

"Nice," Noah said as he strolled across the room to look out the glass wall.

"Byrd?" Kara called as she followed him into the room.

Noah turned and looked up at her. If he had had eyebrows, he would have raised them in question, but seeing that he didn't, he cocked his head instead.

Kara opened her mouth to speak but was interrupted.

"Kara!" A younger woman came rushing from one of the open doors. "God, I'm glad you're here this morning. Explain this!" She held some papers out towards Kara and shook them.

Letting her question go, Kara turned around to address the woman's issue.

Noah turned back to the window to take in the amazing view while he waited for Kara to finish. A strange rumbling in his stomach cramped his gut, and he dropped down to the floor, unsure what was going on. It felt like breakfast had finally hit bottom and did not like being there.

"Poop!" the dragon cried as he took control back from Noah. Byrd looked around until his eyes landed on a beautiful ficus tree tucked in the corner near the elevator. Picking himself up from the floor, he started towards the plant.

"No, Byrd!" Noah cried as the dragon closed on the innocent plant. *"We can't do that here!"*

Byrd stopped and danced in place. *"But, poop!"* He started towards the pot again.

"No, Byrd. We can't poop in the plant!" Noah tried to stop him, but the dragon's desire to relieve the pressure in his gut overrode anything Noah tried.

Byrd paused and shifted from foot to foot. "*But…?*" Memories of relieving himself in the pine trees filled Noah.

"That was different," Noah insisted.

Cocking his head, Byrd looked at the little tree. "*How?*"

Noah let out a sigh. "*Taking a pee outside is nothing like taking a dump in a potted plant. Besides, I think that plant might be fake.*"

Byrd eyed the perfectly round top and lack of fallen leaves and agreed with Noah. "*Fake. But poop!*" The dragon shifted, trying to ease the discomfort in his bowels.

"I'm sure there is a restroom around here somewhere," Noah reassured him. He looked around until he saw something promising. "*Come on.*"

Taking control back from Byrd, Noah headed over to a hall leading off the main lobby. Sure enough, there was a door at the end with a small plaque reading "Restroom." *"Here."* Noah leaned on the door and it swung open, letting them in.

The door opened into the middle of a long, thin room. With the door open, Noah could only see the counter and washbasin at one end of the room. Wiggling around, he shut the door and turned to the toilet in the center of the far wall. It was an odd setup for a public restroom, but it would ensure that no one accidently walked in on someone using the facilities.

Byrd looked at the deep bowl filled with cool water and smacked his dry lips. Most of his breakfast juice had been spilled, and that water looked very refreshing.

"No, Byrd," Noah said, stopping the dragon from dipping his head in the toilet. "*We don't drink out of that.*"

"Why not?" Byrd asked, staring at the clear water.

"Because it's a toilet," Noah answered. "*We don't drink out of the toilet. We poop in it.*"

Byrd cocked his head in thought. "*But… that make water taste like poop!*" He danced around in distress. "*No want poop water!*"

Noah laughed out loud at the absurdity of Byrd's logic. "*It's okay, Byrd,*" he reassured the dragon, "*just hop up there and poop in the toilet, and we'll get a drink out of the sink.*"

Byrd looked back at the bowl at the other end of the room. It was large with a lever that he could easily manipulate. He glanced back at the water readily available, but on Noah's insistence, he gave in. "*Okay.*"

Letting out a sigh of relief, Noah relaxed back and let Byrd do his thing. Life was starting to look up. Now it would be nice if they could just keep things going in that direction.

KARA WATCHED as Byrd wiggled up the steps ahead of her. His butt bounced around in an odd way as he walked. *Is he hurt?* That slip on the steps hadn't looked bad, but then again, it had taken a moment for him to get it together enough to get up the steps. The noise he was letting out sounded like he was in pain. Kara opened her mouth to say something, but her breath caught when the tortured noise took on a familiar rhythm. *Is that… a beat?*

Listening hard, she watched as his back end bounced to the beat of the song he was attempting to hum. He wasn't hurt, he was *dancing*! Astounded, Kara followed him up the steps. In the short time she had known Byrd, he had done many odd things, but dancing just didn't seem like something he would do.

Kara's head rang as she hit upon an idea. *Noah!* Her surprise turned to elation. *This is fantastic!* She knew dragons who had taken years to work through their separation issues. For him to have found some kind of balance so quickly was remarkable, but she had to find a way to verify her assumption. That was the tricky part. Sometimes bringing up separation issues could actually regress a patient's progress. She didn't want to complicate his problems further. Kara mulled over the best way to assess him.

A chirp from the top of the steps drew her from her thoughts. "Come on?"

She looked up at the small dragon waiting at the top of the steps. He twitched and swayed in place as his claws rapped out a rhythm on the tile.

"Sixth floor, right?"

Before she could answer, he hopped up and shoved his way through the door. *That was definitely not Byrd!* The dragon she was coming to know wouldn't have waited. She caught the door and followed him into the room. The best way to find out what she needed to know was to engage him in some kind of conversation. "Byrd?" she called, drawing his attention from the view out the wall of glass and steel.

He turned and looked at her. The cock of his head held a question in it.

"Kara!" Beth called out from her office.

Kara spun to face the woman before she could say anything to the dragon.

Beth bustled out with a handful of papers. "God, I'm glad you're here this morning. Explain this!" She shook the stack.

Taking the papers from her, Kara glanced at the Eternity logo on top of the official-looking pages.

"They're orders," Beth squeaked before Kara could get into the body of the text. "Honest-to-God *orders*. You've been reassigned!" Beth's voice was filled with shock.

"I know," Kara said as she calmly read over the orders Daniel had sent.

Beth stared at her openmouthed. Shock and rage mixed on her face. "When were you going to tell *us*?"

Kara let out a sigh and folded up her orders. "I just found out last night," she explained. "There was an emergency at headquarters that needed a specialist. Daniel called me."

"An *emergency?*" Beth squeaked in outrage. "You're a therapist! What kind of emergency can *you* handle?" She paused as the accusation in her words hit her and she saw how insulting that statement could be. "I mean," she backpedaled, "you deal with long-term treatment, not emergencies."

Kara chuckled. "I thought the same thing. But it turns out, they really did need a specialist. Let me introduce you to Byrd." She turned to where the little dragon had been, but he was gone. "Byrd?"

Beth looked around the empty lobby. "I didn't see anyone."

"He was here just a moment ago," Kara said as she walked over to the spot where she'd last seen him. "He's stuck in his lesser form." Standing where he had been, she scanned the room, looking for where he might have gone. "I swear he was just here." Heading back to the stairwell door, she pulled it open to see if he had gone back in. "Where could he have gone?" The sound of a toilet flushing answered her question. Kara let go of the door and turned towards the sound.

"Is that him?" Beth looked towards the hall that led to the bathroom.

Kara joined her to wait for Byrd to come back. "I sure hope so." Anxiety held her until the door opened and Byrd came out. She sighed in relief as he headed her way. "That's him," she said in relief.

As he drew closer, she watched to see if she could tell what part of his personality was dominant. The bounce in his step and out-of-tune song were gone, but that wasn't much to go by. Her heart dropped when he stopped at the end of the hall to sniff at the carpet. Noah wouldn't enjoy sniffing the floor. Byrd had to be back in charge. "Byrd," she called.

His head popped up at the sound of her voice, and his eyes focused on her.

"Come here. There's someone I'd like you to meet."

It took him a moment to respond, but he nodded his head and came over.

"Byrd, this is Beth Ranchester," Kara said, introducing her coworker.

Beth bent forwards and held her hand out to the small dragon.

Byrd sniffed at it and recoiled. "Stinky woman!" he hissed and backed up.

Straightening quickly, Beth jerked her hand back, surprised by Byrd's outburst.

Kara grabbed Byrd as he backed away from Beth. "Stop, Byrd!" she cried. His tail was already between her legs, and if he went any further, they were both going to end up on the ground.

With her hands on the dragon, she looked up at her upset coworker. "Sorry." She smiled to ease her explanation. "Byrd has issues right now," Kara warned Beth. "It's your perfume. It's very strong, and you know how sensitive dragons can be." Kara's hands ran over Byrd's scales, soothing him.

Beth stood there and glared at them, insulted.

Letting out a frustrated breath, Kara stood up and gave

Beth a sharp look. "Byrd's experiencing a major separation right now. His instincts are in control, and he's likely to react without thinking."

The indignant look on Beth's face was replaced by shock. "Complete separation?"

Kara nodded. "That's why Daniel called me. He needs Byrd whole again. He's…" she let the rest of the sentence hang, unsure how much of Noah's story was classified. The expectant look on Beth's face pushed her on. "…important."

Beth nodded slowly. "That might explain the package that was sent with your orders."

"Package?"

"Yes." Beth turned and started towards Kara's office as she spoke. "The orders came in with the morning mail, but an agent dropped something off a little while ago. He also asked how Noah was." She glanced back to Kara and raised her eyebrow in question. "Who's Noah?"

"Noah Byrd," Kara said, nodding to the dragon at her side. "Who was asking?

Beth made an appreciative noise. "I'm not sure, but he was fine! Tall and handsome. Although he looked like he recently had a bad day."

"That might have been Laurence," Kara guessed as they reached her office. "Did he have several bad bites on his arm?"

"Could have," Beth said, thinking back to the man. "I didn't see anything obvious, but he might have been favoring it a bit."

"That was Laurence," Kara confirmed, opening the door to her office. "Come on, Byrd," she called to the dragon, ushering him inside.

Byrd stopped just inside the doorway before wandering over to the outside wall to check out the view.

Kara shook her head and headed to her desk. Right in the middle was a lumpy manila envelope.

"Who is he?" Beth asked as she followed the pair into the office.

Kara looked up in question.

"The man," Beth said, nodding to the envelope.

"He's a friend of Noah's," Kara explained as she sat down at her desk, letting the subject go. Having just met Laurence yesterday, she really didn't have any answers to give. "When's your first appointment?" she asked, looking up at Beth with imploring eyes.

"Not until after lunch," Beth replied, taking another step into Kara's office.

"I don't know how long Noah's case is going to take. Could you help me sort through my patients? I've got to decide what to do with them until I can get transferred back."

Beth nodded. "Sure. Let me go get my laptop." Turning around, she left.

Kara let out a sigh and looked over at the dragon who was the source of her problems. He'd sat down in front of the glass-and-metal wall and was staring down, watching the cars in the parking lot. He looked so serene sitting there with his tail curled around his feet. Kara closed her eyes to block the sight out. Her dragon was much too content to have him close. He was her patient, and she shouldn't let herself get attached to him. She didn't even know anything about his human side.

Opening her eyes, she looked down at the envelope on her desk. Laying her hands on the heavy paper, she could feel hard objects within the hefty file. *Everything I want to know is right here.* For a moment, she considered ripping it open and sating her curiosity, but she pushed the file to the corner of her desk, out of the way. Right now, she had to deal with her current patients, and dividing them out could take a while. But, once done, she would have all the time she wanted to delve into the enigma that was Noah Dove.

THE SUN SKIMMED across the surface of Kara's keyboard as she sent the last of her files off. She hadn't intended to take so long, but getting her patients organized had proven to be a challenge. Each of the therapists in her office specialized in a different field of mental health. There wasn't much overlap, so finding people willing to take on her patients was harder than she'd first realized. It had taken a fair amount of finagling and a little bribery to get everything covered. What took the most time was updating her patients' portfolios. She was pretty good about documenting everything, but she took a little extra time fleshing out the files. Separation could be a tricky subject, and sometimes the smallest detail could make or break a case.

Pushing her keyboard back, Kara glanced over at her new project. Byrd had been amazingly tolerant as she'd worked. He'd started out staring out the window but got bored with that after a while. Kara thought she was going to have an issue when he started poking around her office, but he quickly settled down on her couch for a nice nap. She watched as his sides rose and fell gently in his sleep. His tail wrapped up between him and the back of the couch to drape over his nose. The tip of it hung over the edge of the cushion and twitched as he dreamed. He was adorable, and she couldn't stop the smile spreading across her face.

Drawing in a deep breath, Kara reached for the package on the corner of her desk. All morning it had been a constant source of both distraction and motivation. Her eyes kept drifting away from her computer to wonder what the lumpy envelope held, but she refused to give in to temptation until she was finished with her work. Now that her last patient was dealt with, she could indulge the curiosity eating at her.

She glanced at Byrd one more time. *Should I wake him for this?* There was no doubt in her mind that the package contained information on Noah Dove. Probably a complete physical and his last psychiatric evaluation. If she were in luck, whoever had put the packet together had included some other insight into Noah's life, as well. If nothing else, a next of kin or emergency contact information. *A family visit could be helpful.* She stopped and considered that thought for a moment. Yes, a visit with someone familiar could help, but if they weren't very accepting, it could do more harm than good. She pushed that prospect off until later in his treatment.

Kara agonized over waking the sleeping dragon for another minute before ripping into the paper without disturbing him. Leaving him asleep would give her a chance to familiarize herself with the information. Besides, Byrd wouldn't be interested in the professional jargon, and Noah would already know what was in his file. Lifting up the end of the envelope, she slid the contents out on the table. In addition to the file she had expected, there was a wallet and a ring of four keys. Moving the keys and wallet back, she picked up the file and flipped it open to find exactly what she'd expected—medical records.

The picture pinned to the top of the page surprised Kara. It wasn't a very flattering image, but it was nothing like the crotchety old man whom she'd expected to see. The handsome face staring out couldn't have been more than twenty-five or thirty years old, but it was hard to gauge his age due to the white streaks in his short red hair. Kara glanced up from the file to the dragon. *How old is this photo?* She looked back down at the small picture. It looked like a photo used in their identifications, and those pictures were usually taken right after boot camp… and weren't always updated as often as they should be. She scanned over the paper, looking for Noah's date of birth.

Kara had to read the date twice to believe her math. The photo wasn't that far out of date! Noah was much younger than she'd expected him to be. She quickly read over the rest of his file to verify the information Daniel had given her. The fact that he was such a high-level mage at such a young age was an outstanding achievement. No wonder he had made it into the ranks of Elite.

Closing the medical records, Kara opened the psychiatric evaluation and poured over it. The results were fairly standard, given his position. Noah was a highly focused and driven individual who had shown exceptional abilities in the fields of magic and problem solving. She scanned over the file before flipping it closed and going back to the medical records. Confusion creased her brow as she searched the files, not finding what she was looking for. There was no emergency contact information listed.

Closing the folder, she looked back over at Byrd. *Don't you have any family?* Kara shook her head and pushed the thought away. There were numerous reasons why a next of kin could have been left out. It was probably an oversight in his paperwork. They could get it sorted out later.

Pushing the files back, Kara picked up Noah's wallet and flipped it open. The official files had given her a glimpse of the type of person she was dealing with, but they were too formal to give her a real feel for Noah as a man. She shuffled through the contents of his billfold, hoping to find something more enlightening.

You could tell a lot about a person by the things they kept in their pockets. Unfortunately, Noah didn't have a lot in his wallet. There were a few credit cards and the usual rewards cards from the local grocery store and gas station, but there were no pictures or keepsakes. There was a small amount of cash tucked in the back, but nothing to shed any light on his personality. She poked through the pockets one more time and came up with a lone condom. Her dragon growled in discontent as she tucked the prophylactic back into place. It didn't like the idea that Noah might have a girlfriend where he would have need for such a thing.

"He's allowed to have a girlfriend," Kara said, trying to hush her dragon. It curled in irritation before settling back down. A wry grin curled the corner of Kara's mouth as she tucked Noah's wallet and keys into her purse. This wasn't the first time her dragon had shown an interest in one of her patients. There was something about a dragon in distress that kicked her protective instincts into overdrive. And Noah was definitely a dragon in distress. She was just going to have to proceed with caution in this case. It wouldn't do to let herself, or her dragon, get any more attached to the man. Once he was better, he would be going back to Daniel and whatever life he'd had before. And that was a very depressing thought.

Letting out a sigh, Kara shut her computer down. There was nothing else she could do here. Now that her other patients were taken care of, she was free to concentrate on Byrd.

Getting up from her chair, she went over to the sleeping dragon. "Hey," she called, rubbing her fingers down his back.

Byrd rumbled in his sleep but didn't wake up.

"Byrd," she called again.

Cracking an eye, Byrd rolled his head and looked at her with one dark pupil.

"It's time to get up." Kara patted his shoulder once more before moving back.

A huge yawn cracked Byrd's jaw as he unfolded himself from the couch.

Kara smiled as she watched him uncoil. "I'm done here. How about we go and do something fun now?"

Byrd blinked at her several times before nodding his head. Hopping off the couch, he stretched his front legs out and gave his wings a good flap before folding them down along his back.

Kara grinned as she gathered up her things. "How would you like to give those wings a proper stretch?" she asked as she held the office door open.

A rumble of agreement came from the dragon as he led the way out the door.

Taking one more look around her office, Kara closed the door and locked it. A note of finality touched her heart as she turned away. With Byrd as her sole patient, she wouldn't see her office for a while. His treatment would be a full-time endeavor, so she wouldn't need the familiar space for meetings or appointments. And Daniel had specifically instructed her to file all of her reports directly to him, which she could do from her computer at home. There was no telling how long it'd be until she saw the place again.

Following the little dragon to the lobby, she waved goodbye to Beth before hitting the button on the elevator. It felt weird leaving without knowing when she would be back, but she shook those thoughts away and concentrated on the rest of the day. The tedious part was done. Now, she was free to take Byrd out and do something relaxing. And, boy, could she use some time to relax.

Chapter 7

"We're here!" Kara said as she pulled the keys from the car.

Noah looked out the front window at the park. He could feel Byrd's excitement rising as he wiggled around in the seat.

"Fly!" Byrd chirped and jumped about.

Amused, Kara tucked her purse under the front seat of the car. "Yes, Byrd. Fly." She climbed from the car and held the door open.

Byrd leaped out and was headed into the grass almost before his feet hit the ground.

"Wait, Byrd!" Noah cried, stopping the dragon before he could rush off. "*Where are we?*" Noah had never seen anything like this place before. It was obviously some kind of park. A wide walking path twisted across an enormous lawn. Workout stations were spaced out along the path, but that wasn't what excited Byrd. Scattered across the lawn was an array of strange shapes on top of tall poles. They looked like giant bubble wands stuck in the ground.

"Fly!" Byrd chirped again.

Kara laughed as she caught up to him. "You go ahead and get started," she said, patting him on the back. "I'm going to go change. I'll join you in a minute."

Byrd rubbed his side up against Kara's leg before turning back towards the park.

"What is this place?" Noah asked again.

Instead of answering, Byrd spread his wings and kicked into the air. A few good beats had them soaring into the sky.

"Byrd!" Noah screeched as the dragon folded his wings and plummeted towards the ground. Adrenaline zinged through their system as the wind rushed over their scales.

At the last moment, Byrd stretched his wings out, catching the air and aiming for the first of the large shapes. He tucked in his wings and shot through the hoop. A quick flap had them turning for the next pole.

Noah's mind reeled as they zipped through the obstacle course. He had flown with dragons before, but it was nothing like the thrill of wind rushing over him now. Flying on his own was exhilarating!

As Byrd finished his first run of the course, he soared up into the air. *"You fly,"* he insisted and released his hold.

Noah freaked as he was thrust into control. It had been thrilling watching as they zoomed around the course, but now it was terrifying. "I don't know how to fly!" he screamed as he clenched his eyes shut and spread his wings out, trying to stop them from plunging to earth. The thin membranes of his wings pulled taunt, catching the wind and leveling out their fall. Noah cracked his eyes open to find they were gliding along above the course.

A flash of red shot up from the ground. It passed so close to him that he wobbled in its wake.

"Kara!" Byrd cried out.

Noah glanced up at a scarlet-red dragon turning loops

in the sky. Carefully, he tilted his wings and banked around towards her. A few hard flaps raised him up to her level. Once he was stable again, he watched the red dragon play.

"Pretty," Byrd said as they watched her twist and twirl in the air.

"She's beautiful," Noah chirped in agreement. He hadn't seen any other dragons since his vision had changed, so he was unprepared for the way the light played off her scales. Their base color was a gorgeous red, but they shimmered and sparkled in the sun. Noah knew that dragon scales had a prismatic effect to them, but seeing it with his enhanced vision was breathtaking. As he cruised past her, he banked again and set himself into a lazy circle around the area where she flew.

After a few more flips, she leveled out and joined Noah in his holding pattern.

Noah couldn't help but be awed by her. Kara wasn't much bigger than he was, but she had an extra-long tail that ended in a fringy tuft.

"Let's race!" she chirped before flapping hard and speeding past him. She swished her tail and swatted him with the fringy end as she passed.

Byrd growled with excitement and shot after her.

Noah relaxed as Byrd chased her through the twists and turns of the obstacle course. With her larger wings, she didn't have to work too hard to keep ahead of them, but Byrd chased after her with a tenacity that kept her from slowing down.

As they came out of the course, she flipped a loop that brought her in line above them. "Again!" she cried and turned to head backwards through the course.

Flipping in air, Byrd took the first loop upside down as he chased her through the shapes again.

Noah's head spun as they raced on. The physical

activity had kicked up his heart rate, but the thrill of chasing Kara heated his blood beyond words. The feelings welling up in Byrd were beyond anything Noah knew. As she flew off, the desire to chase her overwhelmed him. He needed to chase her, to catch her, to claim her. And there was nothing Noah could do to keep Byrd from doing it.

Kara must have sensed some change in Byrd. When she hit the end of the obstacle course, instead of turning around and running it again, she shot straight up in the air as fast as she could go.

Byrd nailed the last hoop and smacked his wings down hard, rocketing up behind her.

With her larger wingspan, Kara pulled away from him, gaining altitude at an incredible rate.

As they rose, the air pressure made Noah's ears pop. He shook off the rampant emotions as warning bells rang in his mind. Memories of some science channel program filtered through his head—something about fighter pilots and rapid changes in altitude. He couldn't remember exactly what the show had said, but he knew it was bad. Noah watched as Kara tore through a thin cloud. They had covered quite a distance, climbing straight up. His breathing grew heavier as he tried to suck in the thinning atmosphere. "*Byrd!*" He tried to get the dragon's attention, but Byrd was too fixated on Kara's form. "*Byrd, stop!*"

"*Mine!*" Byrd cried back, chasing Kara even higher.

Noah tried to regain control to stop the chase, but Byrd wasn't letting go.

Byrd chirped in glee as Kara's wings started to slow and he started to gain on his target.

More warnings rang in Noah's head as they pulled closer to their goal. It wasn't just Kara's wings that were slowing; her head and neck were starting to droop back. Something was definitely not right.

"*Byrd! She's hurt!*"

That got Byrd's attention. The thrill of the chase ran cold as Kara's body stopped going up and started to fall towards them. "*Mine*!" Byrd screeched as they collided. Wrapping his legs around her, they fell in a tangle of wings and tails back towards the park below. Working quickly, Byrd swaddled her in her own wings and clutched her. Wrapping his tail around her, he spread his wings, catching the air. It slowed their fall, but without his tail, he couldn't control where they went.

Tucking his wings, he attempted to aim them for the grassy area behind the obstacle course. Once he was sure of his direction, he spread his wings and flapped as hard as he could to slow their descent. The thought of Kara's limp weight under him gave him the strength he needed to fight gravity's pull. As the ground drew near, Byrd beat his wings until his muscles burned, trying to halt their speed. At the very last second, he tucked in his wings and flipped over, plowing into the ground.

Stars burst behind Noah's eyes as they slid to a stop. Darkness grabbed at him and threatened to pull him down, but he clutched onto Kara and forced himself to stay conscious. It hurt like hell, but he would be damned if he passed out and failed another woman in her time of need.

As they came to rest on the ground, Noah took quick stock of his faculties. Byrd hadn't gotten over onto his back fully, so his wings were bent at a funny angle, but they hadn't been crushed under him. As it was, Noah had taken the brunt of the fall on his shoulder.

Carefully, he unwound his tail from around Kara's lower half and pushed her away from him. His shoulder screamed as he moved it, but it did move. Noah pulled his front leg back, exploring the pain and the range of motion he had in the injured joint. *Probably not broken.* He lay back down to give it a chance to recover from the shock. *Most likely just jarred.* Trying to convince himself he wasn't more hurt, he rolled over to check on Kara. The fact that she hadn't moved worried him more than his battered shoulder. The sound of running feet drew Noah's attention from his fallen companion.

A pair of joggers raced across the park towards him.

Noah stared at them in confusion. He didn't remember seeing anyone in the park when they had first arrived, but Byrd had been so intent on getting in the air, he really hadn't had time to notice much.

The man slowed a few steps back as the woman rushed right up next to Kara and dropped to her knees. "Are you okay?" she gasped.

Noah shifted in pain before speaking. "Yeah," he answered, praying he wasn't lying through his gritted teeth. "I'm good. But Kara..." He looked down at the limp dragon next to him. Gathering up his will, he pushed up from the ground and rubbed his nose into the side of her head. Unable to stop himself, he drew in a deep breath filled with her scent.

Other than the fact that she smelled nice, Noah hadn't really considered Kara's scent before now. Byrd, however, had. Memories of a scent wafted through his brain —*woman* and something soft and floral. It was nice. It was also very similar to what filled his nose now, but this was headier. Muskier. It pulled at his senses and made him want to draw more of the smell in.

Mine!

The declaration bubbled through him from somewhere deep inside. Noah shook his head to drive the thought back so he could check on Kara properly.

"Can I touch your mate?"

Confused, Noah looked up at the woman sitting on the other side of Kara. She held her hands out, waiting for his approval. *She's not my mate!* The words were on the tip of his tongue when a wave of possessiveness hit him. He glanced up at the man standing behind the lady. The need to move over Kara and protect her ate at him, but he pushed it back. Right now, she needed help more than she needed protecting. He nodded his approval to the woman.

Carefully, she reached out to touch Kara.

Noah bit his tongue when a growl rumbled from his chest.

The woman paused and looked up at him.

"Sorry," Noah said, trying to give her an apologetic smile. "It's been a long day."

Nodding her understanding, the woman got back to work unwrapping Kara's wings. She felt along each bone to make sure they weren't broken before folding her wings neatly against her back.

Noah watched her closely as she worked. Every now and then, his eyes would flip up to the man standing behind her. The fact that he hadn't come over sat well with Byrd. The man just stood there with a phone in hand, waiting.

Noah paused and thought about that for a second. It was disconcerting that Byrd wasn't bouncing around trying to take over. "*Byrd? Are you okay?*" he called to the dragon. The answer he got wasn't in words, but Noah understood it perfectly. The high emotions involved in the flight and fall had burned through Byrd's energy. He needed a moment to recover.

An amused snicker rolled out of Noah. The woman looked up at the sound, and Noah buried his nose into Kara's shoulder to hide his mirth. He hadn't meant to laugh. Byrd burning himself out wasn't funny, but it was the feeling of trust that went along with the answer that made him giddy. Byrd trusted him to take care of Kara while he was down. "*I will,*" he promised the dragon. A feeling of contentment filled him before Byrd dropped away from his perception.

"I don't think she's hurt," the woman finally said. "What happened?"

"I'm not sure. She passed out while we were flying," Noah answered.

The woman stared at him for a moment while her hand gently slid back and forth over Kara's neck. "Are you newly bound?"

A negative was poised on Noah's lips, but that feeling of possessiveness filled him again. "Something like that," he answered instead.

A smile curled the woman's lips. "She should be okay," she said, continuing to stroke Kara's scales. "Sometimes that can happen on mating flights."

What the hell did that *mean? We're not mating!* Noah opened his mouth to voice his thought, but a moan from Kara stopped him. He inched closer to her. "Kara?"

She moaned again and rolled her head over towards him.

"Kara?" he called again. "Are you okay?"

She opened her mouth and took a deep breath as if she were in pain.

The possessive side of Noah perked up, ready to do whatever he could to help.

"Yeah," she answered, bending her neck around and bumping into his side.

His ribs protested the pressure, but he refused to move.

She pressed her head into Noah's side. "What happened?" she mumbled against his hide.

The fact that she had buried her head into his side

made Noah worry. He shifted his wing over to shade her head. Bending his neck around, he spoke softly to her. "You passed out."

Kara moaned again as she rolled her head into him harder.

Noah drew in an unsteady breath as he winced in pain. His ribs hurt, but they did not move when she leaned on them. So, probably not broken—just bruised.

"We'll leave you two be."

Noah looked up to find the woman standing up and backing away from Kara.

She dusted the grass off her knees and went to join the man waiting for her. "We'll be around if you need us. Just let her rest for a while. She should be just fine."

"Thank you for your help," Noah said as he laid his head back down on Kara's shoulder. The woman said something else, but Noah didn't hear it. His mind was focused on the woman convalescing next to him.

THE GENTLE CARESS of fingers on scales ushered Kara back into consciousness. A groan of pain slipped out as she resurfaced from the darkness. She ached everywhere. *What the hell happened?*

Movement from her side and the soft call of her name drew her attention. *Byrd?* She cracked the eye on that side to see him, but the light stabbed splinters of agony into her skull and drove another pained sound out. She slammed her eye shut and rolled her head, trying to ease the ache.

"Kara?" he called again. "Are you okay?"

Opening her mouth, she drew in a deep breath, trying to gather the determination to speak. Everything hurt. Knowing that talking would make it worse, she gathered the will to answer. She couldn't leave Byrd to worry about her. "Yeah," she lied. The sound echoed through her skull, making it pound.

She bent her head around to tuck it under her wing but ran into a warm body instead. A familiar scent of musk and male filled her nose, soothing her. She pressed her head into the comforting bulk. Her brain churned on her predicament, but there was too much fog to get it to work right. "What happened?" she asked instead. The heat of the sun cooled as a shadow spread over her head.

"You passed out."

Byrd's voice was soft, but it came from very close to her. She moaned in embarrassment and buried her face deeper in his side. She had passed out. *When was the last time I passed out?* She racked her brain but couldn't come up with an answer. Her constitution had always been very good. The soft voice of a woman made Kara cringe. Not only had she passed out, but she had done it in front of others. Had she been human, she would have been as red as her dragon's scales.

"Thank you for your help," Byrd chirped to the woman before laying his head down on Kara's shoulder.

Kara relaxed under his comforting weight. With her eyes closed, she searched her memory, trying to figure out what had happened. True, the last few days had been taxing, with the move to her new home and Byrd's situation, but it shouldn't have been more than she could handle. She breathed in deep. *No signs of a cold.* The warm scent of dragon and earth filled her, easing some of her pain. She let out the air and pulled in another deep, calming breath. Emotions rolled through, and she suddenly knew what had happened.

How could I be so stupid! she groused as her brain played back over their outing. Coming to the park had been a great idea, but she should never have joined Byrd in the sky. Or at least, she should have let him lead. Running from a male usually kicked up their instincts to chase. Running from one functioning solely on instincts was asking for trouble. And something she should have known not to do.

It wasn't until her second pass through the hoops that she realized her folly. When she glanced back to see Byrd following her, her instincts kicked in. The look on his face ratcheted her hormone levels up, and the urge to run hit her so hard she couldn't stop herself from trying to escape. From there, everything in her memory was a blur of wind, clouds, and sky. She had no recollection of how she'd managed to get down. A sinking feeling in the pit of her stomach told her that her safe return to the ground had everything to do with the dragon beside her.

Rolling her head from his side, she cracked an eye. The sheen of black scales blocked out the sky. Pleasure rolled through her as she recognized the structure of a dark wing protecting her. *He's so sweet!* Realization hit her, and she stomped down on those feeling as hard as she could. *He's my patient; I cannot fall for him!* The warmth in her chest subsided but refused to fully go away. She drew in a deep breath, knowing she was already in dangerous waters. And no matter how much her dragon was pushing her to claim him, Noah didn't need a mate right now. He had enough issues to worry about. Letting her breath out, she pulled her head from under Byrd's wing. The weight on her shoulder shifted as he moved his head to see her.

"Better?"

Kara closed her eyes and considered her condition. The concern in his voice made her heart swell, but she worked to push the emotion away. "A little," she answered. She still felt like someone had beaten her with sticks, but that was starting to fade. She glanced back at Byrd. "How are you?" If her guess was correct, he had saved her from a very nasty fall. But at what expense?

"I'm good," he assured her.

She considered him. He didn't look hurt, but it was hard to tell from her perspective. Nodding her head, she accepted his word, knowing it was probably a lie. No dragon driven by instinct would admit to being hurt around a potential mate. She laid her head back down and closed her eyes. The sun was warm on her scales and did wonders to ease the ache in her body. Byrd's head settled on her shoulder again, making her sigh in pleasure. She may want to deny her growing feelings, but she had to admit there was something comforting in his touch.

After a while, Byrd moved, drawing Kara out of her thoughts. She sighed deeply and lifted her head. "Thanks," she said, not looking back at him. She felt his head lift up off her shoulder. "For saving me." Standing up, she took a few steps forwards before ruffling her wings and tucking them into place along her back.

"You're welcome."

She turned to look at her savior, confused. *You're welcome?* That wasn't the response she'd expected. A brooding dragon would have been possessive, not polite. Could she have possibly read all the signs wrong? She studied him for a moment as he lay on the ground watching her. There was something different about him. She cocked her head, trying to find it. The look in his eyes showed his concern, but he sat there, patiently waiting.

His eyes. Kara looked closer at them. They were lighter than they had been. Byrd's eyes were dark—nearly black—but now they were a warm brown, like root beer in the sunlight. "Byrd?"

The dragon snickered. "He's here somewhere."

Kara's heart skipped a beat in realization as she watched him get up from the ground. "Noah?"

He winced as he stood up. "For the moment."

Shock froze Kara's brain as Noah limped towards her. A million questions flashed through her head. How had this happened? Would it last? Should she call Daniel? Drawn by his limp, the thing most relevant slipped out of her mouth. "You're hurt."

Noah chuckled and limped up next to her. "Just jarred," he reassured her. "I'll be fine in a bit." He moved his shoulder around, stretching it out. A look of pain crossed his face, but he put his leg down, ignoring it. "If you're feeling better, we might want to consider finding something to eat." He started limping towards the parking lot. "It's not uncommon for people to faint from low blood sugar."

Kara stared at him with her mouth open. True, they had skipped out on lunch, but missing a meal had nothing to do with her fainting.

Stopping, he turned back to her. "Unless you need to rest some more?"

She shut her mouth and moved to join him. "No, I think food is a good idea." The look in his eyes told her everything she needed to know. He knew exactly what had happened, but he was giving her an out. By blaming her blood sugar, neither of them would have to acknowledge what had happened. For that, she was grateful. Addressing the issue would bring to light things she really didn't want to face at the moment. Her dragon rumbled at her, but she ignored it.

"So, what do you want for dinner?" she asked as Noah joined her for the walk back to the front of the park. Maybe if she eased into another conversation, she could learn something about him.

"Anything with meat in it," he answered as he limped along. "I could really kill a steak about now."

Kara tipped her head down to hide the amusement lighting her eyes. That was such a typically male statement. But of course, he was male… and a dragon to boot. "I take it you want me to cook?" she teased.

"No… I… um…" he stuttered his way through his answer.

She chuckled. "It's all right." She bumped into his side to show she was teasing him. "I don't mind cooking. Besides, you did earn it."

Noah stopped as they got near the little house that held changing rooms and lockers.

Kara paused and looked at him. He was clearly conflicted about something. She was sure he wanted to deny he had done anything, but he was unable to do it. They would both know it was a lie.

"That was Byrd," he finally said.

Her eyelids drooped over her eyes, and she tipped her head down in amusement. "Then I'll make dinner for Byrd, and you can clean up the mess you guys made in my living room." She turned and left Noah standing there with his mouth hanging open, smiling to herself as she turned the corner into the ladies' changing room. *Noah is fun to tease.*

She shook her head, knowing she shouldn't be teasing him. Now that Noah had resurfaced, she should be picking his brain. They needed to know what had happened to Raven, but right now wasn't a good time to bring up the murder. This was definitely headway in his progress, but pushing him to remember the incident that caused his split could do more damage than good. Better to move slowly than to cause another break in his psyche. Daniel may not be happy about it, but he was just going to have to wait.

Shifting back into her human form, she went to get her things. Tonight, she would dig out her pots and pans and fix him a dinner fit for kings and heroes. And tomorrow, they would head to Noah's house. Then, if he showed more signs of stabilization, she would ask him for the information Daniel needed.

NOAH'S HINDQUARTERS plopped on the ground, and he stared at the doorway where Kara had disappeared. *That woman has sass!* He laughed to himself. He liked a sassy woman. Easing himself down, he relaxed the rest of the way to the ground. The grass was amazingly cool and felt wonderful on his aching body. Letting out a long breath, he closed his eyes and considered his dilemma.

He liked Kara. She was sweet, sassy, and knew how to take care of business. But he wasn't ready to face the things jumbled inside of him. Thankfully, she had taken the out he'd offered. She was a strong woman, and it was clear that her episode had had nothing to do with a lack of food. Had she corrected him, they both would've had to acknowledge what had happened. That would have pulled Byrd back up. Then there would have been hormone-driven emotions involved, and things would have gotten out of hand. Noah didn't know if he could handle that right now.

Worried by the silence of his dragon, Noah reached out, feeling for his other half. The energy of the dragon bubbled inside him, but it was deeper than Noah had ever felt. Obviously, Byrd was still recovering from their outing.

Noah let out a sigh and opened his eyes. He was going to have to figure out a way to deal with his feelings before Byrd came back up. The dragon ramped all of his emotions to a higher level than he was used to. There had been occasions when Noah had teased some of his dragon friends when they'd done something stupid and had blamed it on a hormonal reaction. He regretted it now. Instincts and hormones were nothing to be laughed at.

Drawing in another deep breath, Noah did what he always did when faced with a problem he couldn't think through. Closing his eyes, he emptied his mind and reveled in the world around him. The whisper of the wind through the trees and the warmth of the sun on his scales relaxed him. He breathed deeply, pulling in the scent of grass and dirt. His newly enhanced senses filled him with stimulation like he'd never known. It was overwhelming, but exactly what he needed to settle his emotions.

Slowly, he opened his eyes. His mind was clear. His emotions were calm. And for the first time in a while, he felt centered and ready to do magic. *If only a spell could help.* Thinking of something, he whispered the one healing spell he was good at and aimed it at his aching shoulder. The tingle of magic touched him, but nothing happened. Confused, he said it again, but it still didn't work. Panic hit him as he tried it again to no avail. *My magic!*

He breathed through the panic and tried to regain that calm he'd had a moment before. There had to be a logical explanation for his failure. Many of the mages he knew were dragons, and none of them had ever shown the slightest problem working spells. He huffed in deep gulps of air, but nothing was slowing the terror filling him. His magic couldn't be failing him.

Magic wasn't just Noah's job; it was all he had in life. He'd discovered he was good with it at a very young age, much to his parent's chagrin. They had tried to curb his practice, but it had been a natural thing for Noah. Even through the punishments, he studied all he could. He had stuck with it even through the embarrassment of his father forcing him to shave his head to hide the white in his hair. And Noah's decision to become a mage had caused a rift in his family that nothing could bridge. At eighteen, he had left to face his future alone—a disgrace in his family's eyes. The loss of his magic would be the end of his world.

Lifting his head, he swallowed hard and forced his mind to focus. The healing spell had been an intricate piece of magic. It had taken him a long time to be able to use it on more than just minor scrapes. *Maybe something simple.* Bending his will towards something he knew, Noah picked a simple light spell. As he said the spell out loud, he felt the sizzle of energy, but the ball of fairy light didn't appear before him.

Noah's front feet clenched in distress, driving his claws deep into the dirt. That had been the first spell he'd ever mastered. He'd been using it since the age of six! "Byrd!" he cried out, trying to draw the dragon from where it rested.

Byrd stirred but didn't answer his call.

"Byrd," Noah tried again, shaking his head. He stretched and folded his wings, but his other half did not respond.

"Noah?"

Noah looked up to find Kara coming out of the building towards him. He stood up, then dropped back to the ground. Fear and anxiety paralyzed him in a way he'd never felt before. "My magic," he chirped, shaking his head. His claws kneaded the ground. "I can't."

Kara dropped to the ground in front of him and took hold of his head. She held it so he would look at her. "Noah, what's wrong?"

He swallowed, stretched his wings, and dropped them loose along his sides before he could string the words he was dreading together. "My magic is gone!" He huffed air as the panic attack rolled through him.

"Oh, sweetheart!" Kara said as she rested her cheek on the top of his head and held him. "Just breathe. Everything will be fine."

Indignation burned through the fear. *Fine? How dare she!* He shook her off his head and backed up so he could glare at her. "Fine?" More harsh words bubbled up out of him, but he couldn't make them form right. They came out as chirps and squeaks that only made him madder.

"Noah!" Kara grabbed the crest on either side of his head and forced him to be still. "You're fine," she snapped. "Your magic is fine."

Her words froze him.

"Tell me what happened."

He swallowed twice before he started. "I tried a healing spell." He panted, trying to get the sound coming out of him to be words. "It didn't work." His heart raced with fear.

Kara worked the tips of her fingers into the softer scales on the backside if his boney frill. "Relax," she said, soothing him with both words and touch. "Just calm down, and we will figure this out."

Noah twitched his head in a nod and tried to breathe. He concentrated on the feel of Kara's fingers as they worked the tension from the back of his head. As his heart rate slowed, his breathing evened out and some measure of control returned to him.

"Now, tell me exactly what happened."

Fear crawled back up his spine, but Noah concentrated on Kara's touch and told her what had happened.

"What spells did you use?"

Her words were calm and even, and that helped Noah to remain calm as he told them to her.

"There's your problem."

Noah's eyes hadn't been focusing on anything as he spoke, but this statement pulled his attention up to her face.

A soft smile graced her face. "Spoken spells don't work in dragon form," she explained. "You're using the wrong language."

The wrong language! The truth hit Noah fast and hard. The power he had channeled hadn't taken form because the words he'd used hadn't been correct. Searching his mind, he pulled out a few spells he could do without words. Two were attack spells he had learned in case he was trapped and bound. His favorite was a fire spell that required written runes. But, since he didn't want to hurt or burn anything, he pushed those away and turned to something flashy but significantly less dangerous.

Closing his eyes, he pulled the magic to him and gave it form. As he cast the spell, he listened for Kara's reaction. Her gasp of surprise calmed the fear in his heart. Opening his eyes, he took in the delight on Kara's face as she watched the twinkling fairy lights dance around them. This was the spell he used to wow his dates when they asked him to show them magic. As his own personal adaptation of his first spell, it was something he knew well. Simple, yet elegant.

"This is beautiful," Kara said, releasing her hold on him and sitting back on the grass. She turned her smile from the lights dancing around them to Noah. "See? Your magic works just fine."

Noah looked around at the lights. It wasn't the best job he'd done with the spell, but at least it had worked. Letting out a relieved sigh, he released the spell. The lights twinkled for a moment longer before fading out. "Thank you," he said. They were poor words for the depth of gratitude that he felt, but he lacked for better.

"Think nothing of it," Kara said as she got up from the ground and brushed the dirt from her pants. "You're new to all of this. I'm sure there'll be lots of things you don't know. I'll help you get through it." She smiled softly at him. "That is, after all, why I'm here."

Noah's heart sank at her words, but he nodded his head. *She's my therapist,* he reminded himself. *She's here to do a job and nothing more.* "Thank you anyway." Standing up, he ruffled his wings and settled them to his back where they belonged. "Shall we then?" he asked.

"Of course," Kara said and started towards the car.

Noah limped along behind her. When she opened the door, he climbed in, curled up on the seat, and closed his eyes to rest. He hadn't felt too bad after the fall, but the whole panic attack had burned through what energy he'd had left. Hopefully, Kara wouldn't mind if he took a nap because he wasn't sure if he could keep his eyes open anymore.

Chapter 8

What a day! Kara pulled back the covers on her bed, more than ready to crawl in. And it wasn't even nine o'clock yet. This morning when she'd rolled out, she hadn't expected half of the excitement the day had brought. Some light work, a nice flight, maybe a little progress in Noah's case, but nothing like what she'd gotten. Thankfully, the evening had been much quieter. It had given her a chance to decompress and ponder the events of the day.

Noah's meltdown over his magic had given her more insight into the man she was helping, but not much. He did make his living as a top-level mage. The loss of his powers would cost him his job. But she hadn't witnessed such a severe panic attack in a long time. She'd glanced over his records again but couldn't find anything to suggest he was normally that high strung. Just the fact he ranked as an Elite suggested he wasn't prone to cracking under pressure. And Daniel made sure his men were well tested before sending them into the field. None of his reports had shown any signs of stress after missions.

Since Byrd seemed to be missing, Kara had hoped to talk with Noah for a while, but the day had worn him out. By the time she'd loaded him in the car and gotten on the road, he was sound asleep. He didn't even wake up when she stopped to get provisions for dinner. With as tired as the poor man was, she decided to save the steaks for tomorrow and opted for some chicken sandwiches instead. Noah barely raised his head when the smell of hot food hit him. It took coaxing to get him inside, fed, and tucked into bed. The fact that he was still favoring that front leg bothered her. He may have said it was fine, but if he wasn't moving better in the morning, she was taking him over to see the medic.

A jaw-cracking yawn left Kara shaking her head and snuggling down under her comforter. She blinked her bleary eyes and studied the folds of material she'd hung over her window. They weren't the lovely curtains she had planned, but she hadn't had the chance to go and pick out something nice. And the two tablecloths weren't up there for esthetics. The dark linens would block out some of the morning light. It wasn't an ideal answer, but it beat glaring sun at six AM.

Kara closed her eyes and relaxed. The soft sounds of the night wrapped around her as she drifted on the edge of sleep. She had earned her rest, but her mind held on to the day, playing back choice bits. A soft creak pulled her back from the warm bliss of oblivion. Without moving, she focused on the noise of something moving across the carpet. A hint of fear raced through her as the sound got closer to her bed. *Did I forget to lock the doors?* Her mind raced, but she distinctly remembered locking both the front and back doors. She froze as something plopped onto the bed near her feet. Her heart was racing, yet a warm wave of calm coming from her instincts told her everything was fine. Lifting her head, she looked down at the heavy object on her bed.

A pool of darkness deeper than the surrounding night had gathered in the shape of a dragon on the foot of her bed. It sat there, staring at her with the most forlorn look in its eyes. It whined at her.

"Byrd?" Kara asked as she sat up. There was something about the way he moved that made her sure Noah was not in charge.

The dragon whined again.

Kara pushed her covers down. "What's wrong?"

"Lonely," he chirped.

The sad note in his voice made Kara's heart clench. *How is it possible for him to be lonely?* "Where's Noah?" She scooted down the bed towards him.

"Sleeping," Byrd chirped. He slid his head towards her.

Kara reached out and rubbed her hand over the top of his head. "Why aren't you sleeping? You've had a long day."

Byrd whined and wiggled his way up the bed a little farther. "Scared." A singled tear slipped out of the corner of his eye, breaking Kara's heart.

"Oh, Byrd!" She moved to the foot of the bed and pulled his head up so she could hold him. "Did you have a bad dream?" The broken pieces of her heart were crushed by his next word.

"Raven," he sobbed. His pain was heavy in his voice, and another tear hit her skin. The little diamond was warm as it slipped down inside her shirt.

Clenching her arms around Byrd's head, she held him as tears welled in her eyes. She knew the pain of losing friends and family, but the thought of losing part of herself was unbearable. After a moment, she pushed the dragon back and reached for the end of her covers. A hard yank had them ripped loose from their nice, neat tuck. "Come up here." She held the blankets back for the dragon.

Byrd crawled up the bed until his head rested on her spare pillow.

Kara threw the bedding over him and lay down against him. "Everything will be all right," she said as she ran her fingers over his neck. "Noah will take care of you."

Another whine slipped out of Byrd as he wiggled on the bed.

Kara chewed on her lip for a minute before adding her support. "I'm here for you, too." She knew there would be consequences to committing herself to the distressed dragon, but her instincts told her it was the right thing to do. He needed her, and her dragon would not let it go.

He rumbled in pleasure as he rolled his head over against her.

She traced his scales as she spoke. "I know we're probably poor substitutes for Raven, but you're strong. You'll get through this."

Byrd drew in a deep breath and let it out in a long sigh. "We liked Raven. She nice."

"Noah's nice, too," Kara added. She worried her lip, not sure her words would be enough to lull the hurt from him.

Byrd tilted his head so he could look at her with one eye.

Kara could see the age in that sparkling eye. She took a deep breath, feeling a fool. Most of the time, it was easy to forget what she was dealing with. Byrd's truncated speech patterns and carefree attitude led her to treat him as she would a child or pet, but he was anything but. Byrd was no hatchling to be scolded or coddled, he was ancient. That single eye staring at her from the darkness held things she couldn't imagine. Pleasures and joys to match her best dreams. Horrors and pains with which her worst nightmares couldn't compare. She felt it pull at her, stirring her wild side to answer the call. Her dragon pushed to the surface, and she drew in a gasp of air, trying to hold on to her human form.

Byrd held her gaze for a second longer before blinking and turning away. "Raven wasn't the first. We survived then. We'll survive now."

Panting, Kara held on to herself as her mind reeled. Those words had come from Byrd, but not the Byrd she knew. This was something older, something deeper. She could feel power tingle across her skin where it touched his side. His words echoed in her brain over and over. What did it mean? She lay there, watching Byrd as his breathing evened out. *Who was he?* The only thing Kara really knew about him was that he had been part of Raven Nightingale before her death. Noah had saved him by forming a dragon-heart stone and claiming him. Other than that, Byrd was a mystery.

Raven Nightingale was even more of an enigma. Kara knew she had been an ancient dragon, well respected and influential in the dragon world, but that was it. *How old was she? Where did she come from?* Kara pondered these questions as she relaxed next to Byrd. Ideas played with her mind, driven by Byrd's words. *If Raven wasn't the first, could someone have given Raven her dragon?* Kara made a mental note to look up everything she could find on Raven before going back to her train of thought. *That would explain how Byrd had known how to make a heart stone, but how did he tell Noah? Or did Noah already know?* She pondered that one for a while.

Rolling over, she pressed her back into Byrd's warm side and let the subject go. No matter how hard she forced the questions through her brain, she wasn't going to get an answer without either Byrd or Noah telling her. And then there was the matter of broaching the subject. Asking about the dragon heart meant talking about Raven's death, and she didn't know if Byrd was ready for that yet.

As Kara shifted to get more comfortable, something hard dug into her ribs. She wiggled around until she was able to pull it out. She didn't need light to identify the soft glitter of the diamond tear. Wrapping it in her fist, she tucked her hands up in the hollow of her neck and leaned back against the dragon again. Somewhere in her sheets was another tear.

Kara had never cried diamond tears, but she knew they hurt to shed. Letting out a sigh, she closed her eyes and tried to get to sleep. She would not bring the subject up while Byrd was still grieving for his loss. She would still work to get them into a condition to answer Daniel's questions, but she would not be the one to cause them any more pain.

A THIN BEAM of sun lanced across the room and fell across the head of Kara's bed. She moaned as the light broke into her dreams. Rolling over, she snuggled into the warmth behind her. A soft sigh of pleasure left her as she wiggled closer to the heat source. Her mind recalled her late-night visitor and the reason she had a warm bed this morning. A smile graced her lips as she relaxed. It was nice waking up with a dragon in her bed. They were warm and cozy.

"Morning," she mumbled as she raised her hand to caress Byrd's hide. Her fingers fell on something firm, but it wasn't the hard touch of scales she'd expected. Kara froze as something draped across her, pulling her closer to the solid mass in front of her.

"Good morning."

Kara's eyes popped open in surprise at hearing a human voice. A wide expanse of creamy flesh filled her vision. *Human flesh!* She swallowed hard as she took in the male chest her hand rested on. The pec muscles were well toned, even if the skin was a bit pale. A smattering of red curls dusted across what skin she could see. Carefully, Kara tipped her head back and looked into the face of the man holding her. Her heart skipped as she recognized him from the pictures she had seen yesterday. His root-beer eyes held amusement in them. "Noah?"

He smiled. "For the moment." The tips of his fingers rubbed down her back, easing her tension. His brow furrowed in thought. "I do have a question, though."

Kara looked at him, waiting.

"What happened?"

She cocked her head, not understanding his question.

"I don't remember how I got here."

Kara laughed lightly to herself. "That would be Byrd." This was probably a conversation best had out of bed. She tried to move out of his arms before answering.

Noah's grip on her tightened, pulling her back in against him. "Shhh," he hushed her, holding her in place.

Unsure of what was going on, Kara froze in his arms. Her heart thumped as he curled forwards so his mouth rested against her hair. She drew in a deep breath, trying to calm her heart, but the smell of dragon musk sent trills of excitement down her spine. It had been a long time since someone had held her this close. Her dragon flashed with desire. It liked that Noah held her so tightly.

"Sorry," Noah apologized as his grip on her eased. "Byrd's focused on you." He closed his eyes as if he were concentrating deep inside. "I can feel him back there, just waiting. You stirred him when you moved." He opened his eyes and stared at her. "He likes you."

A light blush colored Kara's cheeks, and she looked down at Noah's chest. "It's instinct," she explained. Her fingers rubbed over his skin as she spoke. "Where is he this morning?"

Noah's head shifted as if he were thinking. "Sleeping, I think." He paused again. "It's hard to tell with him."

Kara smiled. "You're both a little unbalanced at the moment. Things will settle down as you get used to each other."

Noah nodded. "But that still doesn't tell me how I got here." A smile curled the corner of his mouth as he ran his hand down Kara's back. "Not that I'm complaining or anything."

The hint of mischief in his eye sent a shiver of desire through Kara, speeding her pulse along. She ignored it as best she could. "Byrd came in last night, upset." Thoughts of the two dragon tears lost in her sheets cooled the heat in her body. She tried to think of a way to explain how she felt, but the look in his eye softened, telling her he understood.

"Thank you," he said. "For everything."

The blush that had cooled from her skin came back as she looked back down at his chest. Her fingers shifted across his skin again. "You're welcome." She watched his chest rise as he drew in a deep breath. "That's my job," she said, belittling her actions.

Noah snorted.

Kara looked up at him, surprised by his action.

"It's not your job to care."

Offended by his words, Kara shifted back from him as far as the circle of his arms would allow. "I care," she insisted.

"Yes," he said, pulling her back in against him, "but that isn't your job."

Kara opened her mouth to argue but stopped as Noah went on.

"You're supposed to understand. Not care."

She closed her mouth unable to argue. He couldn't have hit the nail harder on the head if he'd tried. As a therapist, she was supposed to analyze her subjects, empathize with their issues, and help them find a solution to their problems. To truly care about someone required emotions she couldn't afford to have. Emotions she worked very hard to keep out of her work. In this case, she had failed miserably.

She looked away from him, unwilling to face the swirls of feelings floating inside her. "So." She changed the subject and looked back at him. "I think I have an idea on how Byrd is taking this, but how about you?"

Noah chuckled. "Oh, you're going to psychoanalyze me now?"

"Well, that *is* my job," she quipped back.

He grinned at her before becoming more serious. His focus moved up and past her as if he were thinking. "I'm dealing." Coming back to meet her eyes, he went on. "Byrd and I are coming to terms."

"And was this part of the terms?" she asked, patting him on the chest.

That smile she was starting to enjoy slipped back across his face. "No. This was a pleasant surprise." His arms tightened around her gently.

Kara reveled in the joy of being held for a second before going back to her line of questioning. "Do you think it will last?"

Noah let out a forlorn sigh. "Probably not." A look of concentration drove the joy from his face. "I don't think

Byrd's ready to give up control yet." He closed his eyes again. "He's quiet right now, but I think that will change very soon."

Nodding, Kara changed the subject again. "You know, Daniel wants to know what happened."

A pained look crossed Noah's face, and he held on to Kara tighter. "I know, but… Not yet." His fingers clenched into the back of her shirt as he gripped her.

"Is it Byrd?" Kara asked, trying to remain calm. His body had tensed up, and his grip was almost painfully tight.

He nodded his head.

"Relax," she ordered. The tingle of magic raced across her skin where he touched her, but he stayed clenched. "Just relax and let go. You won't win in a fight for control against your dragon. It will only make it hurt."

Kara watched as he nodded again and loosened his hold. She took a full breath of air and concentrated on being human as the hum of magic against her skin increased. "It's all right," she soothed him again. As scales rushed over his skin, she pushed out of his arms before his change called her dragon out. A note of panic hit her when he started to shift into his large form, but he squeaked in pain and shrank into his lesser form.

Worry ate at her as he lay on her bed, recovering from the change. "Byrd?" she said softly, reaching for him. He chirped at her in response, but it didn't make any sense. She stared at the black collar wrapped around his neck. The way the thick leather pressed into his scales looked painful. She reached out to remove it but stopped before touching it. He had thrown a fit the last time she'd tried to take it off him. She waffled for a moment before checking it.

"Mine," he gurgled as she touched it, but he didn't scramble away as he'd done before.

"It's all right, Byrd," she said, rubbing her hand down his neck. "I'm not going to take it off."

Slipping her finger under the band, she checked the fit. As her finger touched the backside of the leather, she felt magic zing across her senses. Something in her clicked as a flood of thoughts and emotions filled her mind. She gasped and yanked her hand back from the collar. The feelings subsided as fast as they'd hit, but now she knew why Byrd was protective of the collar and why he and Noah were progressing so quickly. It wasn't just a decorative band. It was a spell. Carefully, she reached back and gripped the leather by the edges. She pulled on it to see how snug it was. It was tighter than she liked, but not tight enough to strangle him. "You let me know if this hurts."

He gurgled something that Kara took to be an affirmative.

"Rest," she said, patting him on the shoulder and flipping her covers back. "I'll be back." She slid out of the bed and dropped the covers over the dragon. Gathering her bathrobe, she pulled it on and headed towards the bathroom. It was going to take her a moment to sort herself out. A flash of light from her carpet caught her attention. A single tear-shaped diamond sparkled in the morning light. She picked it up and cupped it in her hand. It was cool and heavy against her skin.

Closing her hand around the diamond, she lifted it to her chest and headed into the bathroom. As the door clicked shut, she carefully set the gem on the counter where it would be safe. Once Noah and Byrd had worked things out, she'd find the second tear and give them back. Dragon tears were very rare and precious. If he didn't want them, they would fetch an amazing price online.

TAKING KARA'S ADVICE, Noah forced his muscles to relax and let Byrd take over. The pulse of magic swept through him in a familiar way. It was nice, almost comforting, until the pain hit. He squeaked out, unable to make a louder sound past the band of leather strangling the life from him. He tried to move, to rip the leather from his neck, but his limbs were caught between one form and another, virtually unresponsive in his time of distress. The magic moving through him responded to the danger, and the pain in this throat eased. He lay there, gasping for breath.

"Byrd?" Kara called.

Noah tried to answer her, to reassure her, but the words came out all muddled. "*Byrd,*" he called to his dragon. He could feel the dragon's energy pulsing through him, but it hadn't condensed into something he recognized. It was wild and afraid. "*Byrd,*" Noah called again.

The wild energy snapped into something more familiar and focused on Noah.

"It's okay, Byrd," Noah comforted it. "*You're okay.*"

The sharp edge of the fear eased away as the dragon's energy settled. It spiked back up when Kara's fingers touched the collar on his neck, though.

"Mine."

Noah grabbed control before Byrd could lash out. "*Easy,*" he soothed Byrd. "*She won't hurt us.*"

Byrd calmed as Kara's words echoed Noah's.

"She just wants to check to make sure we're okay," Noah reassured the dragon.

Byrd relaxed more as Kara pulled at the collar. A hiccough of magic spasmed through them, but it stopped as quickly as is started.

Noah's mind reeled as he tried to quiet his distressed

dragon while dealing with the wash of emotion that had hit. He didn't know exactly where it had come from, but it lingered against his mind. A mix of concern and worry that he couldn't place.

"You let me know if this hurts."

Kara's words broke into Noah's concentration. He gurgled at her, but his mind was focused on his dragon. There was something off about it, but Noah didn't know what it was. The blanket flipped over him as Kara got up from the bed.

"Rest," she said, patting the covers over him.

Byrd's attention immediately went to Kara as she gathered up her robe.

"Byrd!" Noah snapped at his dragon, drawing it attention away from Kara. *"What's wrong?"*

There was a soft rumble in his chest as the dragon's attention drifted away from Noah and focused on the bathroom door, looking for Kara. Since she wasn't there, it drifted lazily around the room.

Noah chuckled and shifted so he was upright in the bed. *"Are you still asleep?"*

The dragon rumbled at him grumpily.

"Well, you shouldn't have been up so late last night bothering Kara," Noah teased as he wiggled out from under the covers.

"Mine," Byrd rumbled again.

The urge to go back to sleep pushed at Noah, but he shook his head and got out of bed. *"Oh, no. It's time to be up."*

Byrd grumbled at him.

"Besides, I have to go to the bathroom." The pressure in his gut was getting to be uncomfortable.

The dragon's attention shifted to the closed bathroom door.

Noah had the urge to go that way, but he headed towards the hall door instead. *"Kara's in there."*

The soft call of *"Mine"* drifted over his mind again.

"Just leave her alone for a bit. She needs some time to herself." A hint of irritation rose from his dragon, but Noah ignored it as he found his way to the hall bathroom to relieve himself.

It was weird being back in control of his body. Noah could feel Byrd in the back of his mind. The dragon was not happy that they were awake. *"Not a morning person?"* Noah teased.

Byrd growled.

Another soft laugh came out of Noah. *"Let's go see if we can find something to help that."* The thought of coffee crossed Noah's mind.

"Coffee?" Byrd asked.

"It's a hot drink," Noah explained, thinking about his last cup of coffee. It had been in his own kitchen, just a few hours before the dragon gala. He reflected on that as he headed down to the kitchen. He had rinsed out the cup and set it in the sink next to his dinner dishes.

Dread pulled at him. He wasn't sure exactly what day it was, but he knew it had been over a week since he'd last been home. Thankfully, his job kept him too busy to own pets, but he did have some very lovely orchids that needed regular watering. Plus, there was a refrigerator full of food going bad. Then there was the garbage left in the trashcan in his kitchen. *Oh God, there were fish bones in there.* That was going to smell lovely when he got back. Not to mention the cans outside that had been waiting to be taken to the curb after the gala. He groaned out loud. The whole house needed to be checked on. If nothing more than to make sure it hadn't burned down, or that stupid punk from down the street hadn't tried to set up that meth lab in his shed again. There was no getting around it. He needed to ask Kara to go check on his house today.

Letting out a sigh, he turned the corner into Kara's kitchen and stopped. There were still boxes piled around, but someone had been busy putting the room together. Looking around, Noah found what he had hoped to find. A coffeemaker! Finding a heavy plastic box, he pushed it over to the counter and hopped up on it. He studied the coffeemaker to see if he could figure it out. It was just a standard machine. The red marker in the reservoir floated near the twelve-cup line. His heart leaped for joy. *Fantastic! Kara set it up last night.* Reaching out a claw, he carefully punched the power button. In a few seconds, the song of water percolating through the pot reached his ears. *Heavenly!*

"Hungry!" Byrd rumbled.

Noah smiled and hopped down from the box. "Let's see what we can find." He knew that Kara had gone to the grocery store yesterday. There was a vague memory of her bringing in bags, but he'd been so out of it he couldn't recall what she'd gotten. It took a minute to figure out how to wiggle his claws into the crack between the refrigerator doors, but he finally got it open. The fridge was neatly stacked with a few supplies.

"Meat!"

Noah looked at the package that had drawn Byrd's attention. The links of breakfast sausage looked amazing, but they would need to be cooked. Noah shut the door as Byrd protested. "Be still," he reprimanded the dragon. "If we eat it raw, it could make us sick."

Byrd settled down, but he made it known that he was not happy about it.

With a grumpy dragon pressing on his mind, Noah

went to search the cabinets. After opening the first two, he found what he was looking for. A skillet.

Byrd perked up and watched as Noah worked.

Sticking his head into the cabinet, Noah got his mouth around the handle of the pan and eased it out so he wouldn't get his head stuck again. It had been embarrassing the first time Kara had come down to find him with a box on his head. It would be even more so to find him stuck in the cabinet. Successfully removing the pan, he carried it over and set it on the plastic box. "This would be much easier with opposable thumbs."

Either Byrd didn't understand the suggestion or chose to ignore it. He just sat there, waiting for Noah to continue.

Letting out a deep sigh, Noah pushed the plastic box over in front of the stove. He grabbed the skillet handle in his teeth again and hopped onto the box to place the skillet on the burner. "You know, we should probably wait for Kara to come cook for us," he pointed out.

"No!" Byrd snapped at him. *"Mine! Provide!"*

Noah shook his head to stop it from ringing. Apparently, Byrd wasn't willing to wait for Kara's help. Noah wasn't sure what 'provide' meant, but he looked over the controls on the gas stove. They were pretty straightforward, and he had no problem turning the fire on to warm the pan. Hopping down, he went back over to the fridge. He was starting to get the hang of the fine motor control in his front feet, so getting the door open was easier this time.

Without the use of a thumb, it was a little harder to pick up the package, but he tucked his claws around the sausage and carefully lifted it from the shelf. Proud of himself, Noah bumped the door shut and held the package up against his chest as he limped on three legs back to the stove. It took a moment of hopping, but he got the package up on the countertop.

"I need a fork," he said, looking around at the drawers. He was sure he could get the package open with his claws, but the idea of rolling them around in the pan with a claw after walking on the floor wasn't appealing. It didn't take him long to find the silverware, but he couldn't get his claws in the drawer to get just one fork. After a moment of trial and error, Noah learned he had enough dexterity in his tail to wrap around the fork and lift it to where he could grip it in the folds of his claws.

With his newly acquired fork tucked tightly in his front claws, he limped back to the stove. His pan was hot and ready for the sausages. "Are you sure you don't want to wait for Kara?" he asked his dragon again. When the answering angry rumble rattled his chest, Noah smiled and popped open the package. Getting the meat into the pan, Noah lined them up to cook.

"What's this?"

He turned to see Kara coming into the kitchen. "Byrd was hungry," he answered, turning back to the pan.

Kara came over and ran her hand down his neck.

A burst of pleasure rolled up from Byrd, driving Noah to press into her fingers. Her touch felt wonderful on his scales, so he arched his neck, giving her better access.

She scratched him a little harder as she looked over his handiwork. "You could have waited," she said, backing away and heading for one of the high cabinets. "I would have cooked for you."

Byrd growled at that idea. "*Mine! Provide!*"

Noah hunched down as Byrd's words rattled through his mind again. "I suggested that, but Byrd didn't like it," he said as he straightened back up. "I don't think he's much of a morning person." Noah rolled the sausages so they wouldn't burn. "He's grumpy this morning."

Byrd growled at him but settled down at the edge of Noah's perception.

Kara laughed lightly as she poured herself a cup of coffee. "I bet," she said. She held the pot, considering the coffee. "Do you want some?"

"Please," Noah said in a very grateful tone. "I haven't had coffee since before this whole thing began. Besides, it might help some grumpy dragon wake up."

Another growl echoed up from his chest.

A smile curled Kara's lips. "He *is* grumpy." She set the pot down and pulled out another mug, but she stopped and stared at it, confused. "This isn't going to work."

Noah looked up at the mug. No. There was no way he would be able to pick up a mug to drink out of. "A bowl?" he suggested. It would be messy, but he could probably lap the coffee up.

Kara set the mug down. "I have a better idea." Going over to one of her boxes, she rummaged in it for a moment. "How about a straw?" She held up a package of bendable straws.

Noah closed his mouth and sucked. There was enough of a pull that he was pretty sure he could use a straw. "Sure," he chirped, willing to try it. For a hot coffee, he would try just about anything.

"How do you like your coffee?" Kara asked, bringing the pack of straws over to the counter.

"Just some sugar."

Kara poured a cup of coffee and dropped a spoonful of sugar in it. "Two?"

"That sounds good."

She dropped another spoonful in and stirred it around. "Where do you want it?" she asked, popping a straw in the mug.

Dropping his fork to the spoon rest on the stove, Noah

looked around at the available surfaces. Since he couldn't pick up the cup, he would need someplace that he could drink from it comfortably. "How about over here." He hopped down from his box and headed over to another plastic box against the wall.

Kara followed him and set the cup on the lid.

Unable to stop himself, Noah circled Kara, brushing his side gently along her leg. A rumble of contentment sounded from deep in his chest. Turning his attention to the cup, he sat back on his haunches and wrapped his tail around his feet. Leaning forwards, he drew in a deep breath. The smell was amazing. Carefully, he caught the straw in the side of his mouth and sipped at it gingerly. The robust liquid ran across his tongue and down his throat like the nectar of the gods it was. *Man, that's good.* He took another long pull, surprised that he hadn't scalded himself on the beverage. Releasing the straw, he stared at the cup. "It's not hot," he said, confused by the curl of steam rising from it.

Kara laughed. "It is hot."

Noah turned to look at her. She had gone back over to the stove and was rolling the sausages around in the pan.

"It's very hot," she went on, "but what did you expect? You're a dragon." She turned and looked at him, eyes twinkling with amusement. "You were built to breathe fire. You think a little hot coffee's going to bother you?"

Noah looked back down at his cup. The fact that dragons were built to handle heat had never occurred to him. Practically every part of him was fireproof. He took another long pull of the coffee before heading back to the stove.

"How would you like some eggs to go with these sausages?" Kara asked as she finished fishing the meat out of the pan.

"That would be great," Noah answered as he hopped back up on the plastic box. Kara had pushed it out from in front of the stove, but it was still up against the counter. "Can I help?"

Kara laughed again. "You can make sure these don't get away." She set the plate of sausages on the counter next to Noah and went to the refrigerator to get out a carton of eggs. "Dragon claws aren't really designed for handling eggs."

Noah raised his front foot up and wiggled his claws around. "I don't know," he argued. "I'm getting pretty good with these." He reached out and gently lifted the plate from the counter. The sausages started to roll to one side, and he set it down before they fell. "But I might need a little more practice."

Another giggle sounded from Kara as she came back with the eggs. "You would be surprised at what a dragon can do." She cracked an egg over the hot pan. "There are some artists that work solely in dragon form. Says it gets them closer to their wild side."

"I think my wild side is asleep," Noah said, shaking his head back and forth. "He's unusually quiet this morning."

"That's not uncommon," Kara reassured him as she added a second egg. "Do you want these scrambled?"

Noah considered the eggs. He usually like them over easy, but that would make eating them messy. "Over hard is fine."

Kara nodded and added another set of eggs to the pan.

Confused by her words, Noah pushed Kara back into their conversation. "What do you mean it's not uncommon?"

"Only about thirty-four percent of dragons have some internal dialog between their two halves," Kara explained.

"The rest are either so in tune they don't notice their instincts, or they completely ignore the fact they have instincts. Of the thirty-four percent, only one percent experience DID like you have." She flipped the eggs as she spoke.

"DID?"

"Dissociative identity disorder," Kara explained.

Noah cocked his head, confused.

"Multiple personalities." Shutting the fire off, Kara slid the eggs from the pan onto waiting plates and started dividing the sausages.

"That can't be good," Noah said, hopping down from his perch.

"It's not that bad," Kara said as she picked up the plates and headed to the box serving as their table. "Some of the most renowned dragons suffer from DID." She set the plates down and went back for her coffee.

Noah stared at his food, considering her words. "How do they cope?"

"They listen to their dragons," she said, coming back and sitting down on the other side of the box. "As long as they keep that inner dialogue going, there isn't an issue."

"And when they stop listening?"

"Then they end up like you." Kara smiled to ease the truth in her words. "That's where I come in. I help people work out their issues and learn to live with themselves again."

Letting her words sink in, Noah looked down at his plate. The smell made his mouth water. Moving forwards, he went to take a bite but stopped before he could get it in his mouth. He wanted it so bad, but he couldn't force himself to take it. "I really want this, but…"

"Byrd being difficult?" Kara filled in his thought as she cut up her food.

Noah nodded.

"It will be fine," she reassured him. "You're just brooding."

Noah's mouth dropped open as he looked up at Kara. A sense of satisfaction rolled over his shock as she took the first bite of her food. "Brooding!" he chirped. "But… but… brooding is bad!" Horror stories of brooding dragons raced around his mind.

Kara chuckled. "No. Brooding is natural. Every dragon goes through it. Men more than women. But we have our own issues to deal with."

The inside of Noah's mouth went dry as he stared at Kara. He worked his throat, trying to come to terms with this new revelation. "So, what now?"

"What do you mean 'what now'?"

Noah licked the roof of his mouth. "What do I do now?" He had never heard of anything good coming from a brooding dragon. The thought that he was going through it scared the hell out of him.

"There's nothing to do," Kara answered around bites of her food. "You just go on. Eventually, you'll either find a mate, or your system will settle itself out."

"A *mate?*" he chirped. That soft insistence of "*Mine!*" rolled through him, and he suddenly knew what Byrd wanted. He wanted Kara as a mate. "I can't have a *mate*!" Noah cried, shifting his weight back and forth between his front feet in agitation. "I have work and life and… and…"

"Relax," Kara said. "When the time comes for that to happen, you'll figure it out. Besides, when your instincts find the right person, you won't have much of a choice in it. You either follow where your dragon leads you, or he makes your life miserable. Now, eat your food and don't worry about it."

Noah groaned as he looked down at his plate. He knew

what was going to happen. Either he accepted that Byrd wanted Kara for a mate, or he spent the rest of his days stuck in the lesser dragon's form. His stomach protested its empty state, but he still couldn't bring himself to eat. "I can't."

"Yes you can," Kara reassured him. "Look, I'm already done." She tilted her plate to show it off. "If you'll excuse me, I should probably start getting ready for the day." She stood up and picked her dishes up. "Go ahead and eat. I'll be back down in a few minutes."

As Kara deposited her dishes in the sink, the hunger gnawing at Noah's stomach snapped loose. Bending forwards, he snapped up one of the eggs and chomped it down in two bites. It was disconcerting. Just a few seconds before, he couldn't force himself to eat. Now, he couldn't stop himself. Seeing Byrd's hand in this, he gave in to the desire and devoured the plate of food. *Just when I thought I was getting the hang of being a dragon. What next?*

His only answer was a soft snicker from his other half.

THE SIGHT of Noah scarfing down his food worried Kara. He was most definitely brooding. She didn't need to do a blood test on him to tell his hormone levels were way out of balance. They had been jacked up since she met him, but the fact that he couldn't eat until she was done just confirmed her fears. Noah may not realize it yet, but Byrd saw her as a potential mate—a fact that her dragon was pleased with.

"He's my patient," she grumbled to herself as she climbed the steps. The brush of scales against her mind told her that her dragon didn't care. It liked the messed-up little dragon in her kitchen. Biting her lip, Kara went upstairs to get ready for the day. She hadn't really talked to Noah about it, but she planned to take him over to his house today. Not only would it help him relate to his human side more, but it would give her an idea of the man that she was starting to fall for. Only then would she know if she had any hope of saving her heart.

Chapter 9

The heat of the sunbeam felt good on Noah's scales. He stretched out his wings, soaking up the warmth of the rays. Even after his cup of coffee, he hovered on the edge of a sleep driven by warmth and food. The sound of footsteps on the stairs pulled him out of his nap. He opened his eyes as Kara stepped down from the stairs dressed in jeans and a tight-fitting shirt. The red in her top brought out the warm hues in her brown hair, which curled around her shoulders in a way that made his blood sing. A feeling of possessiveness pushed its way into his mind. He shook his head, trying to drive it off, but it clung there, overshadowing his thoughts. "*She is not ours,*" he grumbled at Byrd, but the soft reply of "*Mine*" filled him again. Letting out a deep sigh, he turned his attention back to Kara. "You look very nice."

She smiled at him. "Thank you." Taking the chair he hadn't destroyed, she sat down to put on her shoes.

"Listen," he started. He'd been thinking of a way to ask for her help since he'd finished breakfast. "Is it possible to go check on my house today?"

Kara looked up from her laces. "That's fine." She settled her feet into her shoes and stood up. "I'd planned on taking you over there anyway."

"Good." Noah folded his wings into place and got up from the floor. "I've got some delicate plants that need tending."

Kara grabbed her purse as she headed for the door. "You have a garden?"

"No," he replied, following her out. "Just a few orchids."

"I've never been able to keep orchids alive."

Noah shrugged as she let him into the car. "They're fickle plants, but not really hard to keep once you know what they need," he admitted. "You just have to be consistent with their care, or the whole thing starts to break down."

Kara settled into her side of the car and considered him. "You're a well-organized man."

Noah shrugged again. "Have to be. Magic is a complicated field that requires attention to fine detail. If you aren't organized, you could miss something, and the whole mess could explode in your face. Quite literally." Several incidents early in his career came to mind. Thankfully, he'd pulled through with little more than time off to recuperate and missing eyebrows. There had only been one big explosion that had left him in the hospital, but even that wasn't as bad as it could have been.

The conversation trailed off as they headed out. Noah sat up in the seat, watching the world passing by. He knew this part of town. It wasn't horribly far from where he lived.

"Can I ask you a question?" Kara said, breaking into his wandering thoughts.

"Sure."

"Can you tell me about… your collar?"

A flash of fear and protectiveness bubbled up from Byrd, but Noah reassured him gently. "*She's not going to take it from us. She just wants to know.*" After a moment of indecisiveness from Byrd, the feeling eased.

"You don't have to tell me if you don't want," she added hastily.

"It's all right." Noah took a few short breaths to push the rest of Byrd's fear away. He turned to look at Kara. "I just had to calm Byrd. He's a little protective over it."

Kara threw him a curious glance. "Why?"

"It's a spell."

Kara risked a longer look at him before turning back to the road.

"It binds Byrd and I together."

Opening her mouth, she started to say something but stopped. After another second of thought, she spoke. "That explains a few things."

"Like what?"

She gave him a sidelong glance. "Like how you've made so much progress in such a short time." Kara's hands squeezed the steering wheel as she spoke. "You've made more progress in controlling your dragon than any of my other patients." She peeked at him before looking back out the front window. "What you have accomplished in days usually takes months."

Noah sat there, stunned. "But, how can that be?" He thought over everything he had been through with Byrd. Pain rippled up inside him, but he pushed it away and studied every moment since he had put the collar on. "Could Raven have known she was going to be attacked?"

Byrd keened at him, unable to face the memories of Raven's last hours, but Noah ignored him and concentrated hard on what he could remember. She hadn't been herself that morning. He'd thought it had to do with the collar, but could he have been wrong? The pain and crying from Byrd got worse as he worked his way through his memories, trying to recall any detail that would give him an answer.

"Noah!"

Kara's sharp words yanked him out of his thoughts. The most horrible sound was rattling from his chest, and his eyes burned as if someone had shoved red-hot pokers in them. Kara's arms were wrapped around him, holding his head against her chest. Anguish like he'd never known tightened his chest and made him gasp for breath. Something hard skittered over his cheek and plinked down onto the seat next to Kara. She shushed him and whispered soft words that eased the dragon's pain. After a few minutes, the grief lessened, leaving Byrd spent and Noah feeling like a heel.

"Are you better, sweetheart?" Kara asked as her grip on his head relaxed.

Byrd nodded and shifted back to lie on the seat. Still needing the comfort of touch, his head rested on Kara's leg.

Running her fingers down his back, Kara settled Byrd in place before putting the car in gear and pulling back out into traffic.

"I'm sorry, Byrd," Noah whispered to him and drifted in his guilt. He had been so caught up in studying the moment that he hadn't considered how Byrd would handle it. *"Forgive me?"*

Noah could feel the dragon's energy floating around him. There was a touch of resentment there, but after a few minutes of Kara's soft fingers rubbing over his scales, Noah got his answer.

"Yes." There was a wave of warning that went with the

word.

Noah swallowed. "*We will have to remember this moment,*" he warned.

Byrd's energy swirled with grief. "*We knows.*" Pulling away, Byrd's energy curled up in a ball at the back of Noah's mind, leaving Noah to deal with the pain and exhaustion the episode had caused.

Noah savored it as his punishment and vowed to not put Byrd through that misery again unless it became necessary.

THE REST of the ride to Noah's house was spent in quiet with Kara's fingers rubbing the tension from Noah's neck. For a while, he thought about punishing himself more by moving out of her reach, but her touch soothed Byrd, so he stayed where he was but tried not to enjoy her caress.

Finally, when she pulled into his drive and shut off the car, he sat up. "I'm sorry," he apologized.

Kara turned and glared at him. "As you should be," she snapped. "Your dragon is a sweet and sensitive creature and doesn't deserve to be abused like that. And if you're too much of a knucklehead to see that, I'll—"

"I'm sorry," Noah said a little louder, cutting her off. "It won't happen again."

Kara glared at him for minute longer. "See that it doesn't." Yanking on the handle of her door, she popped it open, got out, and slammed it before Noah could get up.

"She's mad at me," he said to Byrd.

Amusement rolled up from the dragon.

"Laugh it up, fuzzball," Noah snarked. "Her being mad at me is going to get in the way of your mating plans."

Byrd growled at him. The door opened up on the tail end of the rumble.

"What?" Kara asked, looking in at him and surprised by the noise.

Noah got out of the car and stretched. "I'm having an argument with myself," he explained.

Byrd rumbled at him again.

"Someone doesn't like me very much right now."

"Well, that makes two of us," Kara snapped and slammed the car door shut.

The growl from Byrd grew louder.

Noah let out a sigh. What was done was done, and there wasn't anything he could do about it now. Putting the moment of stupidity out of his mind, he turned to look at his home. It looked just the same as it had when he'd left.

Byrd stopped growling at him and glanced around the yard, his curiosity piqued.

"Let's go see what we can find." Noah made his way up to his porch with Kara close behind.

"And how do you expect to get in?" Kara sassed at him.

Noah turned to see her. She had stopped on the steps with her arms crossed over her chest.

"Magic," he chirped, giving her a playful wink.

The surprise on her face delighted Byrd.

Turning back to his front door, Noah studied it for a second. Nothing seemed amiss. The glass storm door was closed tightly, and the door beyond looked secure.

"But you can't do magic in this form," Kara said as she got closer.

Noah tilted his head so he could see her out of one eye. "I don't have to." Going up to the bare wall next to his door, he stood on his hind legs and grabbed at something unseen. With a quick flick of his head he came down with a string clasped tightly in his teeth. He turned to show off the spare house key he'd hidden in plain sight.

Kara gasped at him. "How?" she asked as he brought the key to her.

"A simple illusion spell," Noah answered. "There's a hook up there with a gem holding the spell. Unless you know exactly where it is, you will never see the key hanging there."

Kara looked at the key. "But what if someone bumps into it?"

"Misdirection." He looked up at the wall where the key had been. "If you bumped into it, you might feel something akin to spiderwebs on your hand or shoulder." He looked back at Kara. "Since most people don't like spiders, they will tend to pull away from that feeling and avoid the place they ran into it."

"You are a clever man." Kara held up the key. "But this was entirely unnecessary." She reached in her pocket and pulled out his regular keys.

Noah's mouth dropped open as he stared at his keys. "Where did you get those?" He distinctly remembered his keys being tucked in the inner pocket of his tuxedo jacket —a coat that should still be at Raven's.

"Laurence dropped them off at my office." Kara pulled open the screen door and fitted the key to the lock.

Noah stood there, processing that thought. *What was Laurence doing with my keys?* He thought over the large dragon. Laurence was one of the few people Noah trusted. Noah had even told the man about the trick with his spare key in case Noah blew himself up and didn't make it to work. Again.

Putting together several possibilities, Noah came up with the most likely scenario. Since Daniel had obviously come for him at Raven's maybe they had gone after his things, too, and then brought them to Kara's office so he would have them. But something in that didn't sit right with Noah.

Laurence wouldn't just drop his keys off without making sure Noah got them. He knew Noah had some delicate things in his basement—spells he'd been working on that were either really dangerous or very fragile. Something about the whole idea made his teeth hurt and put him on edge.

"Kara!" Noah cried out as she turned the knob to open the door. "Wait!"

Kara stopped with the unlatched door in her hand, not yet fully open. "What?"

Noah's heart raced as he threw himself into the wood, knocking the handle out of her hand. The door banged into the wall as he leaped in, ready to take down some unknown danger. He scanned his living room and found… nothing.

Kara caught the door before it could swing shut. "Noah?" she called in tentatively. "Are you all right?"

Letting out the breath he'd been holding, Noah relaxed, feeling the fool. "Yeah. I just…" He let his words trail off, not knowing how to explain the overwhelming sensation that someone was lurking in his home, ready to hurt them. He shook his head, driving the irrational fear away. "It's nothing." For a heartbeat, he wished he could use his magic to check the place out. His aura-finding spell would clearly have told him if anyone were hiding inside. He pushed the wish away and turned to Kara. "Just being paranoid."

Coming inside, Kara shut the door behind her. Her eyes swept across his living room. "This is… nice."

Noah looked around, trying to see it as she did. His home wasn't that fancy. It was a simple one-story, brick home in an older neighborhood. The lot it sat on was only three quarters of an acre, but it did have some lovely trees and plenty of outdoor space to work if he needed it. The main reason he'd bought the house was the basement. Uncommon for the area, his basement gave him the room he needed to practice his craft away from the prying eyes of others. It was his safe haven and escape when things got to be too much for him. He shook that thought away and concentrated on his living room.

It was horrible. The carpet was ugly brown shag, and the walls—yellow with age—were in desperate need of repainting. The furniture wasn't much better. A brown couch with the most offensive flower pattern ever created graced the far end of the room with two matching chairs. A china cabinet filled with knickknacks huddled against one wall, while some sort of flowered picture clung to the other. It wasn't a room he was proud of, but he never used it anyway.

"Thanks," he said, leading the way across the living room and into the den. "It came with the house." He glanced back to see how she took that. Her look of confusion made him smile. "It was already like that when I moved in."

That made her brow furrow more.

"The house was in foreclosure when I bought it," he explained. "The couple that lived here were killed in a car wreck, and the bank had repossessed it. I expected their family to come claim some of their stuff, so I left most of the house like it was for the longest time. But no one ever came, and, well, I haven't felt the need to redecorate."

"So you just live with their stuff?" Kara asked, sounding slightly appalled.

Noah shrugged. "Not all of it." Reaching up, he clicked on the light in the den. This was the room he loved.

Quite a lot of time had gone into ripping the horrible carpet out and putting in a beautiful laminate floor. He had chosen a dark blue sectional that was comfortable enough to sleep on and an oak coffee table. On the wall opposite the couch was the biggest television he could possibly find. To the right was a fireplace he never used, and to the left was a wall filled with books on just about everything he could think of.

"Now *this* is nice."

Noah looked back to see the smile on Kara's face.

"Who did your curtains?" She went over to the window and rubbed her hand over the taffeta and gauze drapes strung artfully over his back windows.

"What makes you think I didn't?"

Kara gave him a pointed look that made him laugh.

"One of my ex-girlfriends couldn't stand the blinds I'd hung up," he explained. "Complained that it made it look like a bachelor's pad. So she fixed me up." He hadn't seen anything wrong with bare blinds. As long as they kept the glare off his TV, what did it matter?

"Why'd you break up?" Kara moved away from the window towards the bookcase wall. Her fingers drifted over the spines as she read the titles.

"I wouldn't let her in my basement," Noah answered. "Come on." He turned and headed through the door into his kitchen.

Returning the book she had picked up, Kara followed a few steps behind.

Noah paused to look around the kitchen. Someone had been here since he'd left for the gala. He couldn't see down in the sink, but the dishes he'd left there had been washed and left to dry in the strainer. And from the lack of smell, someone had obviously taken out his trash. He was almost willing to lay money that that same someone had moved the steaks in the refrigerator to the freezer. Only one person could have been responsible for this. Noah searched around until he found what he was looking for. *A note.*

Pinned to the front of his refrigerator was a single sheet of paper with several scrawling marks and Eternity's emblem hastily drawn on it. "Laurence has been here." Noah edged around the kitchen island and headed across the room.

Kara followed closely behind him. "How can you tell?" She glanced around the room.

Noah nodded at the page. "That's his mark." It really wasn't Laurence's mark. It was a simple protection spell Noah liked to use when they went out into the field, but Laurence had given him shit over it and had scrawled the strange symbol on everything of Noah's he could get his hands on. After a while, the joke had gotten old, but Laurence would still tag things with the symbol to draw Noah's attention to them.

Letting out a sigh of relief, Noah turned towards the door in the corner of his kitchen. His feelings hadn't been wrong. Someone had been there after all. Laurence. But it looked like he was long gone. "Could you help me with this, please?" He stopped next to the closed door.

Coming up next him, Kara reached out and opened the door. A set of steps led down into the darkness of his basement.

"You'll need to head down first," Noah explained. "There's a door at the bottom of the steps, too."

Kara gave him a surprised glance, then turned her attention to the dark stairs. "You're going to let me in your basement?"

Noah opened his mouth, surprised that she would even ask, but their conversation from the living room hit him. Of course she would ask. He'd just told her he'd broken up with someone because he wouldn't let them in his space. Noah cocked his head, amused. "You're smart enough to know not to touch anything. She wasn't." Stepping back, he bowed his head, indicating she should lead. "After you, my lady."

Giving him a wary look, she headed down the steps.

Noah held the upper door open until she was most of the way down. "I'm going to have to shut this," he warned. "Just hold on to the banister. The door is right at the bottom of the steps, and seriously, don't touch anything. Some of that stuff can explode if jostled wrong."

Kara made some sort of distressed noise, but Noah ignored it and closed the door, dropping the stairs into total darkness. It was important to keep both doors shut tightly when he was working down here. Some of the spells he played with were dangerous, and he had gone to great lengths to keep them contained. But that only worked if the room stayed sealed. Carefully, he picked his way down the familiar path. He heard Kara rattle the handle on the lower door. "Just push it open, there's a light on the other side," he called down reassuringly.

"It *is* open," she called back through the darkness.

Noah's heart clenched. It shouldn't be dark. His orchids were down here! "Shit." He rushed down the last of the steps. "Just don't touch anything," he warned again as he brushed past Kara into the darkened room. This was not the first time the light over his plants had popped the breaker. Using the trickle of light from the back window and memory, he picked his way between tables and into the far corner where the switch box was.

Rearing up, Noah found the box and snagged the latch with his claw. Pride swelled in his chest. He was getting better with those things. It only took a second to find the thrown breaker, but Noah paused before fixing it. Fear clenched around his heart. The switch wasn't blown. Someone had deliberately turned the lights out.

A male's deep voice cut through the darkness. "Turn it on."

Enraged that someone would violate his space, Noah slammed the switch into place. The bank of lights over his plants flickered to life, blinding him, but he turned around ready to hurt the person who had endangered his plants. He'd spent hundreds of hours getting those suckers to bloom, and he was going to take apart the person who dared hurt them.

"What's the meaning of this?" Noah growled as he came around the end of the last table to face the voice. His heart dropped when he saw the intruder standing just inside the small alcove next to the door. The man was large, but it wasn't the gun in his hand that made Noah's heart race. It was the hand he had around Kara's throat. A growl echoed up from Noah's chest, pushed by his enraged dragon. The muscles in his back legs bunched as he coiled to attack.

"Stop right there!" the man yelled.

Noah's attack froze when the man moved the gun to point at Kara.

"You make one move, and she's dead."

Rocking back into a more comfortable position, Noah held his place on the floor, ready for any opportunity.

"Shift!" the man yelled.

"I can't!" Noah growled.

"He can't!" Kara snapped at the same time.

The man looked from Noah to Kara. "All dragons can shift!" he insisted. "Tell him to shift!" The hand at Kara's throat tightened as he pressed the gun to her temple harder.

"Shift!" The word gurgled out of Kara as she clung to

the man's hand, trying to loosen his hold.

"*I can't!*" Noah yelled again. He felt the dragon's energy swirling around him, but he knew it wouldn't back down enough for him to change to human. Byrd was much too worked up with Kara in danger.

"*Just do it!*" Kara screamed at him.

The man's attention bounced back and forth between them as they yelled.

Noah's pulse raced as he watched the gun drifting away from Kara's head. Hope welled in his heart. If he could distract the man enough, he might be able to close the gap between them. He held a spell in his mind that he could unleash without words.

"*Do it!*" Kara yelled.

The man's head snapped to her, then back to Noah.

As his attention turned, Kara gripped his hand tightly and kicked out. In an amazing feat of flexibility, she got her feet up against the corner of the alcove and shoved with all her might.

Fear raced through Noah's system as he launched himself towards the pair.

The man stumbled to the side and rammed into a metal table filled with an elaborate array of chemistry equipment. The glass contraption rattled. A single tube slipped from its holder and shattered on the table.

Noah closed his eyes and raced towards them as the chemicals in the tube burst into a ball of blue flame. Time slowed as he counted the seconds left in Kara's life. At three, he slammed into the unstable pair, knocking them to the ground. At four, the gun in the man's hand went off, hitting Noah in the chest like a Mack truck, but the bullet skittered off his scales and ricocheted over his shoulder. At five, Noah popped the spell in his mind, sending a wave of energy out into his target. Unfortunately, the man's hand was still on Kara's throat. They were both racked with spasms as the energy coursed through them. At six, the glass array Noah had been using to brew up a very volatile potion exploded, peppering his outstretched wings with licks of white-hot flame and splintered glass. The concussion from the blast pressed him down over the pair on the floor and darkened the corners of his vision.

The screech of his fire alarm went off, pulling him back to consciousness. He struggled to get his limbs working again. Chunks of the flame-retardant ceiling he'd installed crashed down as it buckled under its own weight. The pressure from the blast had shattered the ceiling tiles beyond recognition, but they had done their job. The flames burning on the table and floor hadn't caught on the beams of the ceiling.

A secondary siren screeched to life, driving Noah past his pain. He now had sixty seconds to get out of the room before his state-of-the-art fire-suppression system kicked in and flooded the room with an unhealthy dose of argon gas. It had been one of his many splurges that he'd made while setting up his lab. On the off chance there was an explosion that left him unable to get out, the argon gas would kill him, but it would smother out the flames before they reached something more dangerous. That, in itself, would save the lives of the poor sods sent to save him.

Shaking the shards of glass and fire from his wings, Noah staggered to his feet. He bumped Kara with his nose, but she didn't move. Moving to her waist, he grabbed the back of her pants in his teeth and pulled her off their attacker. The hiss of the gas drove him faster as he backed up. Thankfully, Kara hadn't let the door shut completely, and he was able to drag her into the stairwell and shut the lower door. The hissing noise stopped as the pressure from the argon gas forced the air seal around the door closed.

Noah struggled through the dark until he was next to her. "Kara," he called, rubbing his nose against her.

She moaned in the dark.

"Come on." He nudged her, forcing her to respond. "We have to get out of here." There was good air in here, but the seal wasn't designed to be perfect.

She moaned again.

Noah found her arm and managed to wiggle under her so she was mostly supported on his back.

After a moment of dead weight, she started to help by clutching on to him.

"Hold on," he said as he started up the steps. Every step hurt. His chest hurt from the bullet. His shoulder screamed from where the blast had reinjured it. His wings and back burned from the sharp glass and caustic potion that had been sprayed across him. Focusing his mind, he ignored the pain and pulled on the energy of his dragon. Byrd was screaming at him to keep his mate from harm. He didn't spare a thought to calm Byrd. He used that to force himself up the steps.

The door at the top of the steps was a bit more challenging, but he got it open. The sudden light of his kitchen blinded him, but he crawled his way out, dragging Kara with him. The audible cock of a gun stopped him, and he turned blurry eyes up to find four men standing in his kitchen, weapons drawn.

Byrd screamed at him to fight, to protect his mate, but there was nothing Noah could do. Kara was nearly unconscious, and he hurt beyond words. He struggled to flip Kara off him and lie down over her. At least that way, they couldn't shoot her. Noah released his hold and let Byrd take over. If anything could save them, it was the savage fury of his dragon.

Byrd growled and snapped at the four men as they got

close, but they tackled him, knocking him off Kara. His claws raked across the face of one of the men as his jaws snapped at another. "*Mine!*" he screeched, trying to get free so he could protect his fallen mate. He drew in a breath, stoking the fires deep in his chest, but one of the men slammed his head into the ground, clamping his mouth shut. Smoke rolled out of his nose, but there was no way to release the flames he had heated. They burned in his chest, forcing him to cool them off.

"Do it!" one of the men yelled.

Thrashing, Byrd fought as someone near his tail scraped something hard against the scales on his hip, separating them slightly. The sharp end of a needle slipped between two of the scales and deep into his flesh. His roar of anger was smothered by the man holding his mouth shut. The serum burned as it entered. Red filled his vision, and he kicked hard, flipping the man on his hip away. Another good thrashing tossed one of the men from his side. The rest released him and retreated to a safe distance. Byrd roared at them, but whatever they had injected him with was already working. Unable to stoke his flames to kill his attackers, he staggered over to Kara's limp form and dropped himself on her again. Breathing hard, he spread his wings over her in a vain attempt to protect her. His vision swam as he clutched onto Kara. Thoughts of Raven's death filled his mind, and he keened out his anguish as another of his was lost to these monsters. He glared at the waiting men as his limbs went heavy and numb.

A bare trickle of Noah's consciousness brushed against Byrd's mind. "*They will pay for this.*"

Byrd blinked one last time before the drug stole the last of his strength. "*With their lives.*"

Chapter 10

"We can't kill him," a male voice called out of the darkness Noah's mind swam in. "The boss wants the dragon."

"But that shit killed Spencer!" another enraged voice responded. "He needs to die!"

"I know," the first voice answered, coaxing the second to see reason, "and he will, but this is what we've been working for. We can't kill him yet. The maks need him alive."

Noah bristled at the slur against mages. The term 'maks' was only ever used in the most derogatory way. It was a word he'd often heard from his father growing up. A soft growl echoed up from his chest.

The conversation on the other side of the room fell silent.

"He's awake," the second voice said.

"He can't be awake," the first answered. "It's only been a couple of hours."

"But he growled."

"He's a dragon," the first grumbled. "They do that.

Besides, that drug will keep him from flaming up for the next day or so."

"I fucking hate dragons. They stink!" The man's last words were muffled as if he were covering his face.

The first man laughed. "And here you're working for a man who wants to be one."

"No!" the second one snapped. "I signed on to this project so I could kill the bloody bastards. Fucking blight on society."

Noah forced his breathing to remain even. He felt around and found Byrd's energy hadn't woken up yet. It was a good thing, because his dragon would have been enraged by the man's words.

"You'll get your chance soon enough," the first voice answered again. "When the maks have figured out how to get the dragons out, you can kill as many as you want."

"But what about the shits that want those dragons?"

"We'll worry about that when the time comes." The way the first voice said that clenched Noah's heart.

"Damn he stinks." The scrape of a chair on a bare floor punctuated the man's words. Heavy footsteps echoed across the room as the man got closer. "When the fuck can we get rid of this shit?"

Something hard banged into something metal near Noah's side. He jerked in response as the vibration traveled through the floor.

"He moved!" the man next to him yelled.

"No he didn't," the other voice said. There was another scraping sound and more footsteps.

Noah forced himself to relax. The startling noise had woken Byrd, but the dragon wasn't fully focused yet. "*Be still,*" Noah warned his other half. This brought Byrd into full focus.

Something hard jabbed into Noah's side and pushed at him.

Byrd started to react, but Noah clamped him down. "*Be still,*" he warned again.

"He's still out," the second voice said. The lighter footsteps moved away.

Noah could feel the presence of the first man standing over him, but he remained relaxed. Keeping Byrd from jumping up and trying to tear out the guy's throat took most of his concentration. "*Be still,*" he pleaded again. "*We need a plan before we attack.*"

Byrd didn't like it, but he stopped fighting with Noah.

The man stood over them for a moment longer before turning away.

Noah cracked an eye. Steel bars filled his vision. Shifting his head just slightly, he watched as a short, stout man walked away from him.

"When are they coming to get him?" the man asked as he threw himself into a chair and crossed his arms over his chest.

"As soon as they're done with the girl," the second man answered.

Rage colored the edges of Noah's vision. He clamped his control over Byrd down before the dragon could give away the fact that they were awake. "*Patience,*" he pleaded.

"*Mine!*" Byrd screamed at him.

"*I know,*" Noah soothed him, "*but we need more information before we can save her.*"

Byrd thrashed about in Noah's mind, hating the fact that he was helpless. After a moment, he settled. "*Kill them,*" he growled.

"*We will,*" Noah promised. "*But we need patience and calm right now.*"

"*Mine,*" Byrd growled once more before falling silent.

Now that Byrd was settled, Noah focused his mind on their situation. They were caught. His eye shifted around, taking in their prison. It looked to be a small steel cage. Something you would put a bear or lion in. Beyond that was a mostly empty room, maybe twenty feet by fifteen. The walls were white plasterboard. Nothing remarkable about them. The ceiling was made from soundproof drop-ceiling tiles. There was a long window on one wall, but there were blinds dropped over them. Light leaked through, but it didn't have the quality of sunlight. So, a hallway.

With the environment firmly in mind, Noah concentrated on the two men arguing at the far end of the room. They weren't very remarkable, either. One was short and dressed in what looked like a short-sleeved uniform shirt and dark blue trousers. He had a ball cap pulled on over his muddy brown hair. The other man was taller. He sat relaxed in his chair in jeans and a T-shirt. His feet were kicked out in front of him with his booted feet crossed at the ankles. He tried to pacify the smaller man as they argued. There was something familiar about the smaller man, but Noah couldn't place it. After a moment, the pair fell into a waiting silence.

The smaller man glared at Noah for a while before blowing up. "Fuck!" He jumped up from his chair and started pacing. "I work with these shits all day, every day, and now they want me to sit here and watch this one? Fuck that!" He ripped a knife out of his belt and turned towards Noah. "I'm killing it!"

The second man jumped up and grabbed the first. "Oh, no you're not!" He yanked the knife out of the first man's hand and turned him around. "They need him alive."

"*Fuck!*" the smaller man snapped, "I can't stand it in here!"

"Then let's go get some coffee." The taller man turned them towards the door.

"But—" the other guy protested and turned his head to look at Noah.

"He's not going anywhere," the first man said reassuringly. "He's still asleep. Besides, he can't get out of the cage. It's enchanted."

"Fuckin' maks."

"And you need to chill out for a bit."

With that, the two men disappeared out the door.

Noah lifted his head and watched as their silhouettes passed by the long window.

Byrd growled.

"It's okay," Noah promised. "They're first on our list."

This appeased Byrd.

A quick look around solidified Noah's facts before he started making a plan. First thing on his list was getting out of this cage. Standing up, he leaned against the bars, testing them. From their color, temperature, and the fact they didn't give, Noah guessed they were iron. He might be able to do something with that. Iron wasn't the best material to work magic on, but it wasn't impossible.

Noah chipped his claw scratching at the hard surface. When he had a workable rune scraped onto the metal, he drew in power from the world around him and poured it into the mark. He felt it hit the symbol and skitter away like water on dry ice. The sharp smell of ozone filled the air, making him sneeze. He shook his head, trying to clear it. *They're enchanted.*

Byrd growled at the failed attempt and chomped down on the iron rod. His teeth clicked against the bar but didn't make a dent.

"Stop," Noah called, pulling the dragon back before he broke a tooth. "*There has to be an answer.*" Taking control, Noah searched the cage. He pressed on the walls and ceiling, testing the welds to see if anything would give. Nothing did. Next, he rattled the door, trying the hinges and lock. Both were solidly made.

Noah eyed the padlock. It was just a normal lock, but if the mages had enchanted the cage, they had probably enchanted the lock. If he could find something long enough, he could pick it open, but he would need the dexterity of his fingers. It would be impossible with claws.

He blew out a breath in frustration. He needed to be human to get out. Hell, if he were human, he could spell the lock off. His lock-picking and trap-breaking abilities were some of the main reasons Eternity had hired him in the first place. The fact that he was a natural with magic was a lovely bonus. He sat back on his haunches and prepared himself for the fight he was about to have.

"Byrd," Noah called out to his dragon, "we need to be human."

"No." The dragon's response was fast and firm.

"I can get us out of this cage, but I need my magic to do it. And I can't work magic like this."

"No." The answer was a little slower, but still very firm.

Noah tilted his head down and closed his eyes. He had to get his dragon to agree with him. "Byrd, if we want any hope of saving Kara, we need to get out of this cage. I can do that. But you have to let go."

"Mine." The word came out conflicted as Byrd waffled on his choice.

"Yes." Noah nodded. "We can save her, but we have to go now. Before they come back." Noah didn't know how long it would take the pair to get coffee, but he didn't stand a chance of escaping if they came back before he was free.

"For mine."

Noah felt the dragon's hold release. He breathed out as the familiar tingle of magic rushed over his skin. He let it take him, shifting his form to something more familiar. Opening his eyes, Noah blinked. After being in dragon form for so long, the world looked strange. Duller than it should be. Shaking the feeling away, he sat up and moved towards the door.

The lock was exactly what he'd thought it was—a simple padlock. Wrapping his hands around it, Noah pulled energy from the world around him and aimed it at the lock. He muttered his spell, spinning it into the enchantment already there. Concentrating hard, he pulled the enchantment apart, shredding it free of the metal. When he was done, the lock was still latched, but now it was nothing more than a lock. Pulling his fingers back from the metal, he muttered another spell that ate the heat from the lock. It was a very simple spell, but it super-cooled the steel to a brittle temperature. Leaning back, Noah kicked at the door with his heel. It rattled hard before the latch on the cage gave way. Noah stared at it in shock. He'd expected to have to beat on the door to get the lock to shatter.

Sitting up, he looked at the thin bar that had held the door shut. The pin that held the joint together had snapped in the extreme cold. Someone had forgotten to enchant that one little piece. *Aww, hell. All that work for nothing.* Shaking his head, Noah climbed out of the cage.

The feel of scales pushed against his skin.

"Not yet, Byrd," Noah pleaded as he wrapped his arms around himself. "We need to be human."

A wordless question bubbled up from Byrd.

"To blend in," Noah explained. "We need to find Kara before we transform."

Byrd paused to think about that before backing down.

"Thank you." Standing up, Noah concentrated on what he needed to do. Now that he was free, he needed to find clothing. Being human would let him blend in, but whoever was holding them would probably notice a naked man running around. Voices from the hall drew his attention. The voices of the two men coming back with their coffee.

Racing across the room, Noah slipped behind the door and drew up more power. He whispered the first part of a spell, weaving the energy into something akin to the spell he'd used in his basement, only more lethal.

As the two men came into the room, the shorter one stopped when he saw the empty cage. "He's gone!"

Barking the last line of the spell, Noah leaped out and grabbed both men by their shoulders. Electricity coursed through them, burning out their nervous systems.

The two men dropped without a sound.

Clinging to their shirts, Noah lowered them both to the ground. Carefully, he shut the door in case someone else came by. Byrd coiled in satisfaction as Noah dropped down next to the men and started stripping them. He studied them as he worked, trying not to think of what he was doing. There was something vaguely familiar about the smaller man. He struggled into the taller man's pants as he thought about it. The jeans were much too tight to be comfortable, but the smaller man's clothing would be too short. His shirt, though… that would fit him better than the T-shirt.

As he pulled the work shirt off, something caught his eye—a small symbol embroidered on the dark material. *An infinity symbol with a line through it.* He stared at the dead man. *This guy worked for Eternity!* Flipping the dead man over, Noah grabbed the back of his pants and rolled his belt down. Outrage ate at him. Just on the inside of his pants was an iron-on tag with the man's name and department listed on it. *Lambert. Maintenance.* The man was a goddamned housekeeper at the main office. Noah slammed his hand down on the man's back and ripped the shirt the rest of the way off him. *How the hell could anyone from work be involved with this? They were supposed to protect dragons, not slaughter them!*

Byrd growled his anger, and Noah committed the man's name to memory as he pulled on the shirt and buttoned it up. He tried to button the pants, but they were too tight. Leaving them open, he fluffed the shirt out over the open fly and went to the door. They would stay up for what he needed to do. Glancing back, he considered the men's shoes, but both pairs looked too small for his feet. A second thought occurred to him, and he went back for Lambert's ball cap. He pulled it down tight over his hair and returned to the door.

Easing it open, Noah glanced up and down the hall. No one was around. Pulling the cap low over his eyes, Noah pushed the door open and stepped out. Unsure which way to go, he turned away from the direction the men had gone and walked towards the door at the far end. It opened into a large room. *Wrong way.*

"Mine," Byrd grumbled.

"I know," Noah growled. They needed to find Kara, but he had no idea where to start. Taking a deep breath, he calmed himself and thought. If only he had a way to find people. An idea hit him, and he whispered his aura spell. Blinking a few times, he turned around and surveyed his surroundings. Viewing things on an astral plane took a lot more work than seeing them with his eyes. The energies of living creatures radiated out, unhampered by inanimate objects like walls, but it was harder to judge spatial distance than with normal sight. Thankfully, this was a skill Noah was used to. If the mages were working on getting Kara's dragon out, they would be concentrating hard. He scanned around until he found what he was interested in. A grouping of intense colors. That was where Kara would be.

Byrd growled his impatience.

"Easy," Noah soothed the dragon as he released the spell and blinked the effects away. Contrary to his words, he hurried back into the hall, past the room where he'd been kept. He'd expected a few powerful auras, but what he'd found were a few very determined people surrounded by a haze of auras dense enough that it was hard to distinguish the individuals in the group. They must be working on Kara in a wide area where anyone could watch.

Byrd's anger grew. His mate was being tortured on display, and no one was stopping it!

Noah held on to his dragon but let that anger push him forward. At the end of the hall, he turned right and started looking for a staircase. The grouping of energy had been lower than he was. His feet picked up speed as he searched. When the hall ended in a door, he slammed through it.

The hum of energy stopped him in his tracks. Catching the door, Noah looked around. The path ended abruptly in a railing. To the left was a set of metal steps leading down, but it was the people who captured his attention. Towards one side of the room was a wide space where three men in dark robes stood around a table. Noah didn't have to look to know Kara was laid out on that table. It was the stacks of crates surrounding the area that stopped him from racing down there and killing them all. There had to be twenty people perched on those boxes.

Noah shut the door so it wouldn't slam. Turning around, he rubbed his face, trying to come up with a plan that wouldn't get them both killed. Byrd wanted to leap down there and rip them apart, but Noah held him in check. Jumping into that many people was a surefire way to injury, and he still hurt from yesterday's fall and today's explosion. The last thing he needed was a gunshot wound when he didn't have scales that were mostly impervious.

Byrd pushed for them to shift and attack, but Noah shook his head, vetoing that idea. Even in dragon form, he was too small to take on that many while trying to protect Kara. A thought filtered into his head that made him stop. "How big can you get?" he asked.

Pausing in his fight to get to Kara, Byrd questioned him. *"Big?"*

"Yes," Noah said, staring down into the room. "Raven was large when she took me." He raised his fingers to touch his collar. "If it wasn't for this, how big could we get?" The question floated around inside Noah as Byrd considered his answer.

"Big!"

A vague mass filled Noah's head. He looked down at the room and mapped out his options. There was no way he could sneak in and save her. He could do a massive area spell, but that would take time he wasn't sure he had, plus there was no way to single Kara out. The only answer was a surprise attack on a grand scale. But there were problems with that.

In their grand form, they might be able to take out some of the people, but taking them all out would be tricky.

"We do it!" Byrd piped in.

"But what about Kara?" Noah pointed out. "If even one of them gets through, they could use her to stop us."

Byrd quieted as he thought.

Noah looked around the room. It was a massive warehouse. Shelves filled with crates were everywhere. He could shift and knock stuff over as he attacked. That could possibly distract or injure some of the people. Another shake of the head ruled out that option—his aim would have to be dead on, or the shelves could land on Kara. Their best option was a snatch and grab. Byrd pushed him to go, but Noah held him back for a moment. "We need an out," he explained.

Glancing over the warehouse, Noah got a feel for the space. The room was huge. Most of one end was filled with tall shelves, but the area where the mages were working was open, like a shipping bay. Noah searched the wall and found what he was looking for. A bank of loading docks! Most of the doors were closed, but the one at the far end was open. A guy on a forklift was moving pallets of boxes around, but the truck that would take them hadn't backed up to the opening yet. "Do you see it?" Noah asked.

Byrd growled his positive answer, anxious to get underway.

Noah pushed the waist of his pants down over his hips. "This is a snatch-and-run operation," he warned the dragon. "We aren't going to stay and kill them."

This did not make Byrd happy. "*Eat them!*"

"I know," Noah said. "I'm not sure I want to eat them—kill them, yes—but we don't have time to take them all out." He stared down at the group. He could feel the intensity of the magic building. "We need to get her out of there now."

Byrd grumbled but agreed with Noah. "*Protect Mine.*"

"Yes. Mine first." Noah's fingers touched the leather band at his neck. "Are you ready for this?"

A note of fear passed through Byrd, but the need to save Kara drove it away. "*Yes!*"

Working the clasp on the back, Noah pulled the band off. He gasped as the spell released him. The energy of his dragon snapped away, but Noah reached out and grabbed it. "Stay with me, buddy." He opened himself more, drawing the dragon closer to him. It was a weird sensation, but he held on to Byrd until the power stabilized. Now he knew why Byrd was protective of the collar. It held them together until their bond was settled. Raven hadn't taken him as a mate. She had done this for Byrd.

Pushing that thought away, Noah tucked the collar between his fingers and wrapped it around into his hand. There was no way he was leaving behind something so important. "Ready?"

Byrd growled, more than ready to go.

Pulling loose his shirt, Noah stepped up to the railing. Making the mistake of looking down, he clutched to the handle, rethinking his plan. The fall was impressive.

Byrd rubbed up against his mind, reassuring him.

Noah swallowed and started to climb. He had to jump. The platform was much too small for Byrd to shift on. Taking a deep breath, Noah drew up his courage and leaped out as far as he could. The sensation of falling sent a spike of fear and adrenaline racing through Noah's system.

Byrd loved it.

As they plummeted towards the ground, magic raced over their skin, ripping what was left of the stolen shirt and shifting their shape.

Byrd roared his anger as his wings spread, changing their fall into a glide. Screams rose from the group as Byrd dropped down on top of them. His jaws snapped, crushing one of the mages and slinging him away from Kara. He roared again, sending his surprised victims running in terror. The urge to chase filled him.

"Byrd!" Noah snapped, redirecting the dragon's attention. "*Kara!*"

Refocusing on his goal, Byrd wrapped his front feet around Kara's limp body and beat his wings. Yells and gunshot sounded as he slammed his wings down and leaped into the air. Ramming his shoulder into a shelf, he knocked it over on the scattering people as he shot for the open loading bay. The door was a tight squeeze, but he tucked his wings in and hopped through before the men chasing him could catch up.

Aiming for the sky, Byrd clutched Kara to him and flapped hard.

"No!" screamed Noah, trying to catch Byrd's attention. "*Clouds won't cover us. Drop low.*"

Byrd shifted his course away from the bank of clouds. An attack spell skittered across his scales, just missing him. He tilted his wings to swing away from it.

"Go towards it!" Noah yelled.

Byrd flipped his wings and leaned towards the missed spell. Another spell shot past him in the place where he had been heading.

"Drop to street level."

Folding his wings, Byrd dropped like a rock from the sky. Another spell burst above him. Spreading his wings, he caught the air just before hitting the ground. Zipping past cars, Byrd dodged over streetlamps and power lines.

"Go left!" Noah yelled as they came to a T-junction in the street. "*We need to get off the road!*"

Flapping, Byrd gained some height but kept below the line of the buildings.

Noah searched the ground, looking for a place to land. Going back to Eternity wasn't an option. If this group had agents there, it wasn't safe for any of them. He needed to tell someone. Someone he knew was safe to talk to. A dragon. His mind churned as he ruled out possibilities. Suddenly, something plausible popped into his head. *Where are we?*

Byrd looked around but didn't see anything that looked familiar.

"We should be safe for the moment," Noah guessed. They had come a long way along the roadway. It should be safe to get above the buildings to see where they were. *"Go up."*

Climbing, Byrd got them up where Noah could get the lay of the land.

"That way." Noah pointed to the west. *"Stay just above the buildings,"* he warned. They were probably safe from the mages by now, but, as someone who had taken dragons down before, he knew a spell could be very effective, even over long distances. There was no reason to make themselves a bigger target than necessary.

"Where?" Byrd asked as he skirted around the city.

Noah stared out of Byrd's eyes as the suburb sprawled out in front of them. *"Somewhere safe."* Memories of a pub Laurence was fond of came to mind. Noah had only been there a few times, but the owner was an ex Eternity Elite. If anyone could help, it was him. What other choice did they have? Noah pushed away his fears and prayed his intuition was right.

Chapter 11

A swirl of emotion filled Noah as they drew closer to their destination. The old barn tucked into the trees didn't look like much, but it held one of the few places Noah knew of that was safe… he hoped. The man who ran the tavern, Brigs, had been an Elite in his days in Eternity. That, coupled with the fact that he was an old dragon, made Noah willing to seek out his help.

Having found an employee of Eternity among the enemy had been distressing. If there was one traitor in the group, who was to say there weren't more? A memory tickled at Noah's mind. A man swinging a blackjack at his head. It pained him, but Noah forced the memory into focus. There was something very familiar about the man. Suddenly, things snapped into place. A vision of the same man, standing in the lab back at headquarters flashed into Noah's head, making him nearly drop Kara.

Byrd gurgled his annoyance and clutched his mate tighter.

"Sorry," Noah said, but his mind raced over the memory. It had been just a few days before the gala.

Having forgotten something, Noah had gone back to the lab and had found a man poking around the amulet Daniel had sent for them to study. Noah didn't know the guy by name, but he knew he was a governmental liaison who had been following the case. After vaguely answering the man's questions, Noah had promised to get a full report to Daniel as soon as they had answers. It seemed perfectly normal at the time, seeing as the amulet had been the biggest break in the case.

Looking back, Noah realized he should have known something was amiss. In addition to the questions on their work, the liaison had asked very specific things about the agent who had brought the amulet in. He'd been very interested in knowing the whereabouts of the agent and the condition of his new mate. The fact that Noah couldn't answer him seemed to frustrate the man, but Noah had written it off as stress from the case. It wasn't very long after the liaison had visited that the amulet's power had dissipated.

It wasn't uncommon for magical items to fail after a while, so no one had thought anything of it at the time. But after seeing the man in Raven's home, Noah knew he had done something to break the spell on the piece. This had to be brought to Daniel's attention.

A growl from Byrd drew Noah's mind away from the betrayal. They were coming up on their destination fast. There was a note of unease in Byrd's heart.

Noah pushed his doubts away so he could soothe Byrd. *"It's all right. Brigs will help us."*

"Mine," Byrd rumbled as a warning, but he landed on the ground just outside the open barn doors. He very carefully laid Kara out on the ground before stepping back and bumping her with his nose.

"Yes, Byrd. Ours," Noah agreed. There was no way he

was going to fight with Byrd about his claim on Kara. The dragon had made up its mind, and Noah knew enough about dragons to know resisting that pull would be pointless. Besides, he was really starting to like her. *"Now, back down so I can help her."*

Byrd growled again but pulled back, leaving Noah in control.

Noah stared down at her limp form, but there wasn't much he could do. "I can't work like this," he rumbled.

Another growl issued from the dragon, but Byrd recoiled further, allowing Noah to shift into his human form.

Noah shivered as the scales withdrew, leaving his naked skin exposed to the air. He looked down at his hands to find the collar still caught between his fingers. "Good job," Noah praised the dragon.

"Mine," the dragon answered.

A smile turned Noah's mouth as he wrapped the leather band around his wrist twice and buckled it in place. It was the best place he could think of storing the item without pockets. He wanted it secure, but needed it easily accessible in case he needed to whip it off and transform again.

This pleased Byrd.

Now that the collar was secure, Noah focused on Kara. She was much too still for his liking. Squatting beside her, he searched for the pulse in her neck. A steady beat met his fingers, driving some of the anxiety from his heart.

"Kara," he called as he rubbed the back of his curled fingers against her cheek. "Wake up." His free hand rested on her chest as he checked her breathing. It was shallow, but steady.

"Kara," he called again, patting her cheek.

She breathed in deeply and let out a light moan, but she didn't move.

"Come on," he said as he gathered her in his arms. "Let's get you inside." The feel of magic tingled against his skin as he held her close.

Byrd growled at the familiar spell.

"Easy buddy," Noah said, quieting his dragon as he crossed the hard-packed dirt to the barn. "We'll fix her, but we need to get inside first." He could have started breaking the spells on her right there, but the barn offered a more secure location. Besides, he was naked. Working sky-clad had never bothered Noah, but he usually didn't do it in a public location. Claiming that he was a dragon may help with some public decency laws, but that would only get you so far. He wanted to avoid any contact with the law for the moment.

Heading into the barn, Noah paused to look around. There wasn't very much here. Along one wall were shelves stacked with supplies for the pub below. At the far end of the room was a door. Noah wasn't exactly sure what was behind it, but he did recall his friends telling him that Brigs had some kind of storage place for the dragons that frequented the pub. The middle of the floor was empty, but there was enough space that he could shift if necessary.

Heading to the back wall, Noah found an empty spot and sat with his back against the wood. He shifted around until he had Kara cradled comfortably in his lap with her head cushioned in the curve of his shoulder. Tipping his head over, he laid his cheek on top of her head and relaxed. The feel of the magic on Kara rubbed against his senses, and he opened himself to them. Usually, this was a very dangerous thing to do, but Noah had been picking spells apart since he was young.

The power of the spells washed over him, and he

grabbed them before they could take effect. He pulled at the magic, studying it. Dissecting it. *Two spells.*

Byrd growled in anger.

"Shh…" Noah calmed his dragon before the magic got loose.

Byrd backed down to let Noah work.

Noah concentrated on the spells. The first one was familiar—a simple sleeping spell that Noah himself had used on occasion. Finding the weak point in the magic, he broke the spell and let it fall away. It would take a moment for the power to fully release Kara, but that would have no lasting effects. The second spell, however, worried him. It was very similar to the spell he'd used to free Byrd from Raven, but there was an issue. The spell had separated the dragon's energy from Kara, but it hadn't gathered that energy into a form that could be used.

Pulling at the magic, Noah found a weak spot and broke the spell away.

Kara drew in a sharp breath but didn't wake.

Noah nuzzled her hair, comforting her for a moment before getting back to work.

Byrd fidgeted in worry. They both could feel the damage the spell had done to Kara. They may have saved her life, but it was going to take a real miracle to save her dragon.

WARMTH SURROUNDED Kara as she regained consciousness. The urge to snuggle down into it hit her, and she shifted to get closer. Pain ripped through her, driving out a gasp. She tensed as the world came into sharp focus and all she found was pain. "Aaah," she moaned, trying to make the hurting stop. Her head pounded and her back ached, but that was nothing compared to the burning sensation racing along her limbs. A grimace twisted her face as she turned into the warmth holding her.

"Shh."

Freezing, she cracked an eye to find she was buried into a familiar chest. Again. Noah's voice washed over her as he whispered a line of random sounds. The pain racing through her eased, leaving her limp in his arms.

"Kara?" he called to her softly.

Kara opened her eyes and tilted her head back to look up at him. "Hi," she said as a soft smile turned the corner of her mouth. "We really need to stop meeting like this."

Noah chucked at the teasing. "You know, under other circumstances, I wouldn't mind meeting you like this more often." He squeezed her lightly.

Her heart skipped as a blush bloomed on her cheeks.

"But seriously." The humor drained from Noah's voice. "How do you feel?"

How do I feel? Many things raced through Kara's mind. She ached, but she wasn't really hurting anymore. Her emotions were stirred by the man holding her, but she didn't think that was what he wanted to know about. There was something that was bothering her, but she couldn't put her finger on it. "I feel… off." She looked for a good way to explain what she felt. "Hollow."

"Quiet and alone?" Noah asked.

"Yes," Kara answered. That was exactly what she felt. Something inside her was still when it should be active. Fear crawled at her. "What happened?"

Noah's hand rubbed down her back, calming her. "We were captured," he explained calmly. "I'm sorry. Byrd and I couldn't stop them at the house."

The fear in Kara spread and she twisted around to see where they were. *A barn.* Her mind started to race.

"Shh…" Noah hushed her again, drawing her attention back to him. "We're safe for now," he reassured her. "Byrd and I got out shortly after waking up, but…" he trailed off.

"But what?" The fact that he had stopped scared the hell out of her. *What did they do?*

Noah sighed deeply. "They had already started to remove your dragon by the time we got to you."

Terror ripped through Kara. That was the still spot in her. Her dragon was gone! She gasped as the panic started to set in.

"Shh…" Noah said again, holding her tighter. "Calm down. We got you before they could get it out."

Kara's breath came fast and hard as she held on to him. "But it's not there."

"It's there," Noah reassured her as he ran his hand over her hair. "Byrd can feel it. It's just separated."

Tears bloomed in Kara's eyes. The idea of losing her dragon was crippling. The band of Noah's arms around her got tighter.

"Mine. We fix."

The way those words rumbled up from Noah's chest broke through Kara's fear. The cadence and tone were wrong. She pulled back and looked up into his eyes. They were dark and slitted, like a dragon's. *Byrd.* Then the color and shape shifted back to the lovely brown that was Noah.

"But how?" Noah asked. His eyes lost their focus as he talked with his dragon.

Kara held her breath as she watched his inner conversation play on his face. The color of his eyes flashed back and forth from nearly black to brown as his two halves worked things out.

"Will that work?" Noah asked and paused. He shook his head. "Could it go back on its own?" Another pause as his eyes changed again. "I see, but…" His eyes came into focus, and he looked down at her. "That would be up to her." His eyes darkened again. "No, Byrd. It's up to her."

"What?" Kara asked, interrupting their conversation. It was infuriating to only get one half of the argument.

Noah let out a sigh. "We've got a couple of options." He paused as his eyes flashed dark again. "No, Byrd, it's *her* choice." Letting out another sigh, he refocused his eyes on Kara again. "Sorry about that."

"Go on," Kara encouraged him.

"As I said, you have options," Noah started again. "Your dragon is still there, but it's been pulled loose." He flinched as if something in his head hurt but went on with closed eyes and a pained voice. "If you wait, there's a chance that things will settle down and you'll reconnect with your dragon." Noah opened his eyes and continued. "This option could take time and leave space between you and your dragon. Byrd doesn't like that."

"I can tell," Kara said as she raised her hand and rested it on his chest.

Noah gave her a halfhearted grin and went on. "The second option is to let Byrd help you reconnect with your dragon."

Kara stared at him in shock. "He can do that?"

"He thinks he can."

"How?" Her mind reeled at the possibilities.

"Well," Noah looked past her. His face showed how uncomfortable he was to share this. "It's going to require a bond."

That shocked Kara. She stared at him in disbelief until his eyes came back to meet hers.

"Byrd thinks he can lead your dragon back to where it

belongs, but he needs a connection to it, and… well, it's likely that connection would be permanent."

Kara stared at the apologetic look on Noah's face as she wrapped her mind around that. The only bond she knew of that would connect two dragons was a mating bond. "Are you asking me to be your mate?"

Noah blushed and looked away. "Well… um, that is…" His mouth opened and closed. "I know we don't know each other…"

A smile worked its way onto Kara's face. Noah was adorable when he was flustered. Raising her hand up, she turned his head back to look at her. "Is this what Byrd wants?"

His eyes flashed dark again as his arms tightened around her. "Mine!"

The sudden embrace squeezed a laugh out of Kara as it warmed her heart. In the short time she'd known him, she had come to care greatly about the dragon. "All right, Byrd," she said. "I'll be your mate."

A purr of pleasure rumbled through him.

"On one condition."

The sound stopped as Byrd perked up to listen.

"You have to let Noah be in charge most of the time." It was a little dirty, forcing the dragon to relent to Noah, but mated dragons tended to be very instinctual—especially during the first few months of their bonding. This would give Noah some chance of holding his own against his dragon.

Byrd gave out an irritated rumble before it dropped to a soft purr. "Mine," he said softly as he rubbed his chin on the top of her head.

Kara giggled and turned her face up to rub into his chin. "Mine," she echoed, claiming him. Even though she couldn't reach her dragon, she knew this was what her instinctual side wanted. After a moment of cuddling, she pulled back. "Now, give me back Noah."

Byrd let out a chirp before dumping Noah back into control. His eyes flashed back to brown, and Noah gasped.

"Fun dealing with dragons, isn't it?"

"Yeah," Noah scoffed. "Like riding a roller coaster without a seatbelt."

Kara snickered.

The look on Noah's face grew solemn. "Seriously, if you don't want to do this—"

Kara raised her hand and covered his mouth before he could go on. "Stop," she said, "I've already agreed to it, and if you back out now, you'll upset Byrd. And you don't know miserable until your dragon is unhappy with you." Kara could see dread in Noah's widened eyes. "Besides, Byrd is cute and sweet. I like him, and my dragon will be happy about it." Sadness swam through her. "Well, she will if I get her back."

"Hey," Noah called, bringing her back from the edge of despair. "We'll fix this."

A sad smile turned her mouth. "I hope so." Fear of never reaching her dragon ate at her heart, and she looked away from him to blink back tears.

Pulling herself together, she met his eyes again. "Either way, I'll gladly take Byrd as a mate." She poked Noah in the chest. "You, on the other hand, are going to have to work for it," she said, trying to lighten the mood.

Noah chuckled. "I'll do my best."

She scoffed at him. "You can start by never zapping me again. That hurt."

A light laugh slipped from him. "I promise. Never again."

Drawing in a deep breath, Kara turned the conversation to where it needed to go. "So, how's this going to work? Do we need to find someone to help us share a scale?"

"No." Noah shook his head and shifted her around. He held up his arm and showed her the black band that had been around his neck. "We're going to try this first."

Kara gave it a confused look. "Your collar?"

Noah nodded and unwound it from his arm. "Raven gave this to me." His voice was tinged with sorrow. "I thought it was designed to join us as mates, but looking back, I think she knew something was up."

"Wait," Kara said, shocked. "You and Raven were a couple?"

Red crept across Noah's cheeks. "Not really," he said.

Kara cocked an eyebrow at his embarrassment and waited for him to go on.

"She kind of… um…kidnapped me during her…" Noah paused, cleared his throat, and mumbled something.

"During her what?" Kara asked. She had a pretty good idea where he was going with this, but he looked so cute all flustered and red.

He muttered again.

Smiling, Kara cocked her head, waiting for him to speak up.

The red on his cheeks darkened. "Her fertile period," he growled through clenched teeth. "She kidnapped me during her fertile period."

Pity and mirth filled her eye. "I'm sorry." She tried to sound comforting but failed. Just the idea of a mage being kidnapped by a dragon in heat made her want to laugh.

Noah rolled his eyes and nodded his head. "Anyway. The collar didn't do what I thought it would."

That dried Kara's amusement up. She looked at the black strip of leather. "Then what did it do?"

"I thought it was meant to bind me to Raven," he explained, "but it bound me to Byrd instead."

"It's a link to Byrd!" Kara gasped as things fell into place. *This explains everything.* Noah had made leaps and bounds in his progress because he'd been helped along by magic. Possibilities flashed through her head. This could be an answer for some of her harder cases. If she could just find a way to duplicate it.

"Yes."

Noah's voice pulled her back from her epiphany.

"Byrd feels that we can use this to link us together." He hesitated. "But he warned me that it's more than a simple mating bond. It's a…" he paused and cocked his head as if he were listening. "Byrd doesn't know exactly what it will do, but he believes it will give him access to your dragon." Tilting his head, Noah looked back into her eyes. "It's your choice." He held the collar out to her.

Nerves made Kara's palms damp as she reached for the collar. Taking it, she looked at the black dragon tooled into the leather. It was beautifully wrought. With trembling hands, she wrapped the leather around her neck and fastened it in place.

A tingle of magic washed across her mind. The strange sensation made her head swim. Leaning into Noah's chest, she shut her eyes and held on as the world moved in strange ways. Scales brushed against her insides. That sensation was something she was familiar with, but these scales were strange. They were dark and decisively male.

"Mine."

The word radiated through her, making her toes curl with desire.

"Yes, Byrd," Noah's voice called in her head. "*Ours. Now go do what you're here to do.*"

Byrd's energy brushed against her mind in a loving

caress before racing off through her. Heat bloomed on her skin as her heart sped up.

"Easy there," Noah said, holding her to him. "I've got you."

Kara gasped and opened her eyes to look up at him. His voice had echoed in her head as he spoke. Spikes of desire shivered through her, warming her in places deep inside. She had a feeling that Byrd was responsible for her sudden urges, but she didn't care. Giving in to them, she reached up, grabbed his head, and pulled it down to her. Surprise flashed across his face as she crushed her lips to his. She could feel the passion ignite inside of him as his arms tightened around her and he kissed her back.

A roar of celebration echoed through them both. A secondary roar followed.

Kara's heart leaped for joy as the power of her dragon returned. Tears rolled down her cheeks as she sobbed out her emotions. Joy, relief, and desire overwhelmed her.

Noah pulled back from the kiss. "Shh." Running his fingers up through her hair, he pulled her head in against his chest and held her. "You're all right." He rocked her for a moment as Byrd finished freeing her dragon. "Come on Byrd," Noah called, pulling his dragon from her.

Byrd brushed against her mind one last time before slipping away.

As Noah pulled the collar from her throat, the feel of the magic racing through her stopped. Her dragon writhed in pleasure at being back where it belonged, but there was something else there, too. At the very edge of her mind, she could still feel Byrd's presence. Byrd had been right. Whatever he'd done to free her dragon had left a lasting connection.

Sniffling back her tears, she pushed away from Noah and looked up at him. Concern showed on his face, but she didn't know what to say to him. For a moment, they had been connected. She had felt his thoughts, his feelings, and seen into his soul. And he had shared hers. It overwhelmed her that a man she'd just met could care so deeply for her. He hadn't said it, but she had felt it in him. Something needed to be said. Kara opened her mouth, unsure what part of her emotionally driven thoughts would come out, but the sound of a door opening stopped her.

A man stepped out and looked at them. "Hello?"

Kara froze as Noah's eyes went black and his attention snapped up to the intruder. A rumble of anger rose up from his chest as he tensed, ready to protect his mate.

"*Byrd!*" Kara yelled, grabbing his face and pulling it down to look at her.

His eyes locked with hers.

She swallowed hard as swirls of black scales rushed over his skin. "Be calm!" she ordered him. "He's not here to hurt us." Her fingers relaxed, and she petted him. "Now, give me back Noah."

Byrd rumbled in anger, unwilling to back down.

Kara gave him a pointed look. "You promised."

A sneer turned his lip.

She ran her fingers through his hair, scratching across his scalp. "Everything is fine," she soothed him. "Give me back Noah, and I promise, if he tries to hurt us, you can eat him."

Byrd groaned in pleasure as his eyes rolled back. "Mine," he growled one last time before retreating and leaving Noah slumped over her, panting.

Gathering his head in her arms, she hushed him. "You're all right." The scales that had tried to work their way out had receded. "Just breathe. A bonded dragon is a protective dragon."

"A bonded dragon is a grumpy dragon," Noah snarked back.

Kara laughed but was glad to see that his color was returning to normal. "Sometimes."

"Someone said they saw a dragon land," the man at the door said as he stepped into the barn, "but I wasn't expecting this." He kept his distance as he walked over to the shelves. "You look like you have a bit of a situation on your hands." Picking up a blanket, he turned back to face them. "Is there something I can do to help?" He shook the blanket out and held it in front of him as he approached. A warning rumbled up from Byrd, but the man ignored it as he held the blanket out for Kara to take.

"Easy," Kara said, touching Noah's chest. She reached out and accepted the blanket from the man.

He squatted down so he was eye level with Noah. "I'm Brigs. Is there someone I can call for you?"

Unsure how to answer, Kara turned back to Noah.

His eyes were back to brown and flashed with recognition. "Daniel. Can you get me Daniel Callaghan?"

"Aye," Brigs said, standing up and stepping away. "But it'll take him a minute to get here." He paused at the door and looked back. "Who should I tell him is calling?"

"Don't," Noah answered.

Kara's head jerked around to look at him, shocked that he wouldn't answer.

"Just tell him to come alone and don't tell anyone. Eternity's been compromised."

Kara turned back to look at Brigs.

He stood at the door with a serious look on his face. "I'll find you some clothes while you wait." With that, he turned and disappeared back through the door.

Kara's mind reeled as she turned back to Noah.

"What?" There was no way she could have heard him right.

Noah swallowed before looking down at her. "Someone at Eternity is responsible for Raven's death."

That was a blow she hadn't seen coming. Kara sat in his lap, completely lost for words. Eternity was the only hope they'd had of stopping these people. What were they going to do now?

THIS DAY *just keeps getting better and better.* Kara cuddled into Noah's side, trying to process the tale he was spinning. It was unbelievable that someone who'd sworn to protect dragons was out trying to kill them and harvest their dragons.

Daniel sat on the other side of the booth, quietly absorbing the information. As Noah finished, Daniel leaned back. "I see."

Kara bristled with anger. After being given all of this damning information, all he could say was 'I see'? Noah's arm squeezed her against him, keeping her from blowing up.

"What are we going to do?" Noah asked.

Daniel let out a long sigh. "Well, first, we need to get you and Miss Rose somewhere safe. You obviously can't go back to your place."

"Yeah, about that," Noah interrupted him.

Daniel held up his hand, stopping Noah. "I'm already on it. The fire department called me when they responded to your alarm and found a dead body. We were all very relieved to find it was not you. Laurence is going to see what he can do to save your flowers."

Kara felt Noah go rigid.

"Did Laurence drop my keys off at Kara's office?"

A concerned look crossed Daniel's face. "No."

"Then who'd you send?"

"I didn't." Daniel frowned. "We couldn't find your things at Raven's, but Laurence assured us you had spare keys at home. Your wallet, however, is still missing."

"No, it's not," Kara piped up. "I have it. It was with the files you sent over yesterday."

Daniel went very still.

Kara's heart skipped as Noah held her tighter to his side. Something told her that Daniel was not responsible for pulling Noah's records.

"I think it's best if we get you both out of here." Daniel slid out of the booth. "Now." He went over to the bar and rapped on it. "Brigs!"

Noah stood and pulled Kara up with him. He wrapped the blanket Brigs had given them around both of them.

Standing in the curve of his arm, Kara looked out over the pub. The warm tones of the wood lit by hurricane lamps should have made the mostly empty room feel safe, but after hearing Noah's tale, Kara's eyes checked every corner for enemies. The only other people in the bar were two old men tucked into a corner, but they were deeply involved in a conversation and paid them no mind. But even they made Kara nervous.

"All right," Daniel called, bringing Kara's attention back to him. "Go with Brigs."

Kara turned her eyes to the owner of the bar.

Noah held her in place for a moment. "Do you trust him?"

Kara's gaze shifted between Noah and Daniel, waiting to see what the man said.

Daniel stood tall as he answered. "With the life of the King himself."

Nodding, Noah pulled Kara into motion. "Come on." He followed Brigs out the back door.

Swallowing hard, Kara went with him. Worry ate at her. With Eternity compromised, their only hope lay with a man neither of them knew.

Byrd brushed against her mind, calming her anxiety.

A smile turned the corners of Kara's mouth and she leaned into Noah, trusting his judgment. If Daniel's promise swayed Byrd, then she would join them in facing whatever was to come. It was time to let someone else worry about things for a while. Besides, she had the man at her side to worry about. Noah may have found a balance with Byrd for the moment, but they were far from what she would call stable. And she was going to enjoy exploring every detail of his dual personality, helping him through his issues, and taking her time learning all of his facets, both mental and physical.

Epilogue

Scrawling his signature on the bottom of the page, Daniel let out a deep sigh and tucked the sheet into the folder. His report was not going to make Kyle happy. He'd suspected they had traitors in their midst, but to have two discovered in such a short time was horrifying. Now that he had a written account of everything Noah had said, he was going to have to get busy searching through his ranks to see who could be trusted. But that was going to be a monumental task. Eternity employed thousands of people.

Daniel pondered his problem for a moment. The best place to start would be with the maintenance man Noah had killed. Maybe his file would give Daniel some clues as to where to search. *Or maybe I should start with the bureaucrat who sabotaged the necklace.* That was an idea. He was still alive, and Daniel knew about what time he'd been in the lab. He could pull the surveillance tapes and easily identify the man. There were only twenty or so governmental liaisons with access to that lab, and Noah had given a fairly good description of him.

A knock at the door drew Daniel out of his thoughts. Looking up, he saw Kyle standing there, waiting for him.

"My Lord." Daniel stood up as Kyle came into the room. He froze as another man followed the king in.

"I'm here for your report on Noah Dove," Kyle said.

Daniel's hand rested on the folder as he stared at the pair. Something didn't sit right with him. He had never seen the king's companion before. "About that," he said, picking up the completed file and sliding it into the drawer on his desk. "I haven't finished it yet."

Kyle looked shocked. "But I thought you said you were working on it?"

"I am," Daniel said as he turned to pull another file from the shelf next to his desk. "But something more important came up." He flipped it open and pretended to read.

"What's more important than stopping these murders?" the man following Kyle snapped.

Daniel looked up from his file. "Things." He closed the file and set it on his desk. "And who would you be?"

The man stood rigid, on the edge of anger.

"This is Alan Meyer," Kyle said, holding his hand out to the man. "Mr. Meyer is here as a representative for Minister Driskell."

Daniel ran the man's name through his memory. "Minister Driskell? But doesn't he already have a liaison?" He was definitely sure the senator had another man on staff. A name popped into his head. "Eugene Henderson?"

Alan shook his head. "Eugene is Minister Lewis's aide. Christopher Turner was Minister Driskell's aide, but he had a family emergency. I'm taking over for him as of today."

"Ah." Daniel nodded his head as he remembered the man. Tall, dark hair, dark eyes, well built. He paused as things clicked into place. Christopher Turner fit the description Noah had given of the man who had been in the lab. Daniel licked his lips as his mouth went dry. "I do hope everything's okay," he said, trying to cover his alarm.

"He'll be fine," Alan assured him. "He just needed to be with his family for a while."

Daniel drew in a deep breath as Alan spoke. The only scent of dragon on the air was himself and Kyle. Alan smelled human, but he'd have to get closer to be sure. He cast a quick glance at Kyle, but the king didn't seem bothered by the new man.

"Enough about Chris." Alan waved Daniel's worry away and pointed him back to the conversation at hand. "What can you tell us about Noah Dove?"

Daniel cocked his eye at Kyle, but the king just shrugged. He turned his attention back to Alan. "I haven't had time to complete my report, but Noah is safe. He's working through his issues with Miss Rose, and I hope to have a detailed account of what happened in the very near future."

"You don't have that information already?" Alan pressed.

Daniel glared at the man. "Pushing a dragon who's experienced a catastrophic rift the way Noah did can cause them to regress in their treatment."

"Very true," Kyle said, backing Daniel up.

Alan's spine went rigid. "When do you think you will have his report?"

"Soon," Daniel said vaguely.

Indignation made Alan bristle. "Don't you care that an Ancient was killed while she was in this man's care?" he snapped. "What did he see? What does he know?" The man's eyes narrowed. "What aren't you telling us?"

"I will get you my report as soon as it's ready," Daniel said as smoothly as he could.

"We cannot wait for your report!" Alan demanded, "Where is Noah now?"

"He's in the care of a qualified psychiatrist who is helping him reconnect with his dragon," Daniel answered in a very even tone. "He will be available for questioning when she deems he is stable enough for it."

Kyle raised an eyebrow in question at Daniel.

Daniel locked eyes with him for a moment before looking back at the upset aide.

"Where is he?" Alan tried again.

"Can you get me some kind of report by this evening?" Kyle asked before Daniel could answer Alan's question.

Daniel gave the king a sharp nod. "I will have something for you by this evening."

"Very good," Kyle answered before Alan could protest. "Then I will expect a report on my desk by midnight." He turned and ushered the angry aide out.

Pausing in the doorway, he gave Daniel a knowing look. "And I need you to be available for a flight later. I need to stretch my wings." With that, he followed the aide out and shut Daniel's door.

Daniel let out a sigh of relief. Kyle knew something was up. His request was proof that he understood Daniel was holding back. A flight would give them time to talk alone.

Moving the file on his desk back to the shelf, Daniel took out the file he'd finished on Noah. He couldn't turn this in to the king. It would end up in Eternity's records, where anyone with the right security clearance could find it. He set the file on his desk and went to his safe.

Opening the door, he considered the contents. He had planned on giving everything to Kyle and letting the king decide what to do with it, but Alan had changed that. Taking out the files he had on Michael and Alex, he placed them on the desk with Noah's. He pulled out the heart and added it to the pile. They would have to be removed from the building. This case was no longer safe within the walls of any Eternity location.

Making a decision he knew would get him in trouble, he shoved everything into his bag and slung it over his shoulder. Shutting off his computer, he went to his door and checked the hall. *Clear.* Moving quickly, he made his way towards the main gate. It was nearly quitting time, and no one but Alan would question Daniel leaving a little early.

A quick nod to the guard at the gate saw him out of the building and away. Now, he just had to make sure he wasn't followed. He had to get this information somewhere safe, and he could only think of one location. The Dragon's Wing. Brigs would know where to hide this stuff away until Daniel could figure out what to do with it. Then, for the safety of his men, he had to find a way to falsify all of the documents pertaining to the biggest case they'd ever had and pray that Kyle would understand and not have him court-martialed and hung for treason.

Acknowledgments

It's always hard when I come to the end of a book. I've fussed with it for weeks, lost sleep over it, chopped whole sections out to rewrite, and added thing in I never intended. It's been bounced to betas and editors so many times, by the time I get the finished manuscript back before formatting I want nothing to do with it. But when the book ends and the characters are finally done arguing in my head, it lonely.

My friends have gone off and told me what they wanted me to know and left me to deal with my real life again. I don't know what to do in those days after the final words are typed. Should I take a break and finally do those dishes that have piled up in the sink? Or maybe slay the laundry monster that's creeping down the hall? But before I can do any of that, I have to take a moment and thank all of those people that make a book possible.

So many people have helped me along the way. My mom and Aunt Laura are still my best beta readers. You make sure I stay on track. Kathy-Lynn and Ethan have both listened to me and encouraged me when things haven't gone the way I wanted. Krys and Karl, the loves of my life, need to be thanked for putting up with me while I slave away on my computer (No I'm not just playing on Facebook all day). The ladies of CTP have always been outstanding and encouraging. My editors are wonderful and put up with me when I'm difficult, and for that I need to thank them. And of course I need to thank my readers. Without you this book would not have happened. Thank you for supporting me and I hope you all have enjoyed the ride as much as I have.

Also by Julie Wetzel

The Kindling Flames Series

Book 1: Kindling Flames: Gathering Tinder

Book 2: Kindling Flames: Flying Sparks

Book 3: Kindling Flames: Smoke Rising

Book 4: Kindling Flames: Stolen Fire

Book 5 : Kindling Flames: Burning Nights

Book 6: Kindling Flames: Blazing Moon

Novella: Kindling Flames: Granting Wishes

Boxed Set: Kindling Flames Boxed Set #1

Boxed Set: Kindling Flames Boxed Set #2

Dragon's Of Eternity Series

Book 1: On the Accidental Wings of Dragons

Book 2: For the Memory of Dragons

Book 3: For the Heart of Dragons

Book 4: A Castle for Dragons

Book 5: For the Kingdom of Dragons

Stand Alone

White Lies

About the Author

Originally from Ohio, Julie always dreamed of a job in science. Either shooting for the stars or delving into the mysteries of volcanoes. But, life never leads where you expect. In 2007, she moved to Mississippi to be with her significant other.

Now a mother of a hyperactive red headed boy, what time she's not chasing down dirty socks and unsticking toys from the ceiling is spent crafting worlds readers can get lost in. Julie is a self-proclaimed bibliophile and lover of big words. She likes hiking, frogs, interesting earrings, and a plethora of other fun things.

Subscribe to Julie Wetzel's newsletter to get news on her new titles, giveaways, events, and more!

Julie would love to hear from you!

www.juliewetzel.com

juliectp@gmail.com

Also by Julie Wetzel

The Kindling Flames Series

Book 1: Kindling Flames: Gathering Tinder

Book 2: Kindling Flames: Flying Sparks

Book 3: Kindling Flames: Smoke Rising

Book 4: Kindling Flames: Stolen Fire

Book 5 : Kindling Flames: Burning Nights

Book 6: Kindling Flames: Blazing Moon

Novella: Kindling Flames: Granting Wishes

Boxed Set: Kindling Flames Boxed Set #1

Boxed Set: Kindling Flames Boxed Set #2

Dragon's Of Eternity Series

Book 1: On the Accidental Wings of Dragons

Book 2: For the Memory of Dragons

Book 3: For the Heart of Dragons

Book 4: A Castle for Dragons

Book 5: For the Kingdom of Dragons

Stand Alone

White Lies

Made in the USA
Columbia, SC
14 February 2023

12286168R00133